'Welcome to the world, Sophie Maria.'
Well done, Julie and David!

Acknowledgements

Thanks again to Hugo, my editor, and Vanessa, my agent, for all their hard work and helpful advice.

Thanks also are due to my writing friends, Edna and Sandy; what would I do without you two?

A big 'Hi' to Lizzie, Ayo and fellow members of *Mystery Women*, for providing such encouragement and support.

I must also mention Jennifer, a fellow member of Murder Must Advertise, and Diana, Pauline and all at Houston SinC. I've learned a lot, guys. Thanks.

Last, but certainly not least, love to my husband, George; Mark, Bel, Bronte and Mia, the Aussie branch of the family; Louise, Kerry, Dan and Lulu (the garage doors and the gate still look wonderful, Kerry – you're a star.) Love also to Maria, Ed, Michelle, Andrew, Alex and Aimee, and the Cornish crew, John, Sue and Rebecca.

G.E.

Prologue

DI Joseph Rafferty grasped his great-nephew in a tentative embrace and stared down at the newborn's red face.

From where he sat, next to his sleeping niece, Gemma's, hospital bed, the slant of the early-morning sun across the baby's head lit up what looked suspiciously like ginger hair. For all that the auburn-haired Rafferty thought, *Poor little blighter*, at this discovery – he was ridiculously pleased to see that, like him, Gemma's baby had a dimple in his chin. He felt an instant, warm glow of kinship with this new soul; a glow immediately cooled by his sister Maggie's teasing comment.

'He looks a natural, doesn't he, Ma? Maybe it'll be your and Abra's turn for parenthood next, Joe. Certainly, at *your* age, you don't want to leave it much longer, or you'll be getting your pension when the kid wants you to stump up for college.'

Rafferty shifted uneasily in his chair as Kitty Rafferty and Maggie exchanged conspiratorial glances.

From the other side of the bed, Rafferty felt the critical gaze of Mrs Newson, the baby's other proud grandmother.

'He doesn't look a natural to me,' she remarked, lemon-tart. Her acid advice for Rafferty was: 'You should support his head. Not let it dangle like an onion over a Frenchman's bike. You'll damage the poor child's neck. Or turn him in to a vegetable for real.'

When Rafferty didn't respond to Mrs Newson's instructions

quickly enough, she stood up, said, 'Here, give him to me,' and practically snatched the baby from his arms.

Rafferty was too startled to voice a protest; not so his mother. But before his ma had a chance to get the protest past her lips, from the corner of his eye he saw his sister Maggie give Ma a quick dig in her well-padded ribs. It made Kitty Rafferty clamp her lips on the protest.

But while her protest might remain unspoken, it was far from unfelt. Rafferty, at least, had no difficulty in sensing the waves of indignation his ma was directing across the bed's slightly soiled lemon duvet.

Oh God, he thought, as he caught the amused eye of one of the other three new mothers in the small side ward. He wished himself elsewhere . . . somewhere . . . *anywhere*. Even to learn he was to head up another traumatic murder case would be preferable to this current angst-ridden situation. At least it would give him the excuse he needed to make his escape before the two sides came to blows over the new baby.

Because, although Wayne Newson, the young father of Gemma's new son, wanted nothing to do with the child, Wayne's mother was determined that wouldn't mean she was shut out. After all, the baby wasn't only his sister Maggie's first grandchild, he was Linda Newson's, too.

Rafferty, whose ears, during Gemma's pregnancy, had resounded to the stereophonic blasts of indignation from both his ma and his sister about the backsliding Wayne, was only too aware that because of Wayne, neither of them liked Mrs Newson's insistence on being acknowledged as the child's paternal grandmother. Any more than they'd liked the way Linda Newson – after being apprised via the neighbourhood grapevine of the appearance of an ambulance outside Gemma's home, the herald of another imminent new arrival – had just turned up after the birth to stake her claim. But as it seemed the obliviously sleeping Gemma hadn't voiced any objections, in spite of their natural anger at the way Wayne had treated Gemma, Ma and Maggie were obliged to bite their tongues rather than Mrs Newson.

Exhausted after her ordeal, Gemma was well out of it and mercifully unaware of the simmering emotions surrounding her.

Rafferty wished for a similar blissful oblivion. He glanced surreptitiously at his watch and sighed. Shortly after his arrival at Elmhurst General's maternity ward, Maggie had told him that Gemma would be going home the following day. A pity she hadn't thought of telling me that sooner, he thought.

Of course, this child was the first of the next generation to be born to any of Rafferty's large collection of nephews and nieces, so it came as a surprise to learn how quickly newly delivered mothers were discharged from hospital. If he had realized, he'd have waited and visited Gemma and the baby at his sister's house; at least there he'd have been able to avoid both Mrs Newson's acerbic tongue and the tension between the rival camps.

He wished Gemma would wake up, so he could offer congratulations. Or commiserations. He wasn't entirely sure which, in the circumstances. But, as Gemma was an unmarried teenage mother faced with responsibility for a new life, Rafferty felt that *commiserations* would be more appropriate. And at least if she woke up it would mean he would be in with a chance of escaping this simmering little gathering before hostilities commenced.

Behind him, on the worn linoleum, he heard the clump of institutional footwear. He turned and saw the ward sister approaching. She took a swift inventory of the ward's visitors. Rafferty, suspecting she was about to tell them they were contravening some hospital rule restricting visitor numbers, opened his mouth to volunteer himself for ejection when she saved him the trouble.

'Is there an Inspector Rafferty here?' she asked.

Eagerly, Rafferty met the sister's eye and said, 'That's

me.' He hoped no one else but him noticed that his voice rose up, Aussie-style, at the end, as he sniffed the heady aroma of freedom in the air.

'There's a call for you from a Sergeant Llewellyn. You can take it in my office.'

Saved by the bell, Rafferty thought. Llewellyn would not have contacted him at the hospital unless it was for something urgent.

As he rose, Rafferty kept a tight clamp on his too-expressive features in case eagerness to leave should make its mark. He followed the ward sister out the door of the small side ward, past the fire extinguisher and the notice asking visitors to turn their mobiles off, and walked the few paces to her next-door office before his ma, Maggie or Mrs Newson had the opportunity to express their disapproval that his work should intrude even here.

'Sorry to have to ring you at the hospital,' Llewellyn said as Rafferty picked up the receiver and said hello.

'Think nothing of it,' Rafferty said magnanimously. 'It's the reason I told the station where to find me, after all.'

'How is your niece?'

Reassured that Gemma and the baby were both doing well, Llewellyn went on. 'We may have a new murder case. An elderly lady's been found in her home with fatal head injuries. The injuries look to me unlikely to have been caused by a fall. My first instinct is that she was hit over the head after she disturbed an intruder. I'm still at the scene. It's that sheltered housing block on Priory Way, opposite Priory Park. Parkview Apartments.'

Rafferty knew the place. As Llewellyn had said, the apartments were opposite the park the local council had created from the grounds of the ruined priory – a building that was a bricks and mortar victim of an earlier, Tudor, age of violence and vandalism. Parkview Apartments were in a quiet part of Elmhurst. Near enough to the centre of town to walk to the shops; they were ideally situated for the elderly.

As he listened to Llewellyn's voice with its urgent summons, he reflected on the incongruity of receiving a call to a scene of violent death while at the bedside of a newly delivered mother. But in the midst of life, mortal man must still outface death, he reminded himself. Perhaps his ma, sister and Mrs Newson would accept this argument without complaint, he mused, even as he doubted the possibility.

He asked Llewellyn, 'You've set the wheels in motion?'

Llewellyn confirmed it. 'Smales and PC Green are here with me at the apartments. The Scenes of Crime team and Dr Dally are on their way. How soon will you be able to get here?'

'I'll come now.' He added, attempting to inject a note of virtuous self-sacrifice in to his voice, though he doubted it fooled Llewellyn, who had heard all about the current Rafferty family situation, 'Of course I'll come now.'

Whether his virtue was real or feigned, the need for him to leave was plain enough. He had no choice. He just hoped his family saw it that way.

He kept his responses to Llewellyn's news brief and circumspect. Aware of his family's listening ears on the other side of the thin partition wall, he made sure his words revealed nothing that could be used against him in a kangaroo court.

As he thanked the ward sister and left her office, through the glass window of Gemma's side ward, he caught the raised eyebrows and the exchanged glances of Gemma's visiting family; they made him feel even guiltier. Not only was he sinning by commission, in a few minutes, by leaving, he would also sin by *omission*, an omission made worse by virtue of the fact he'd only arrived ten minutes ago. The last to arrive and the first to leave . . .

If the three ladies gathered like some witches' coven around Gemma's bed let him off with a caution, he'd be doing well, though his conscience wasn't so forgiving.

Already it had started to nag that he should seem to rejoice at the elderly victim's violent death. To placate it, he sent up a silent prayer for her passing.

Rafferty felt more simmering vibes of disapproval greet his reappearance at his niece's bedside. Always the party-pooper, Rafferty, he muttered to himself sotto voce, before he apologetically confirmed what, to judge from their expressions, his fellow visitors had already guessed.

'I have to go. I'll try to pop in again later. Tell Gemma that, and give her my love and congratulations.' In an attempt to lighten the atmosphere, he said, half-jokingly, 'Tell Gemma I shall expect her to name the baby Joseph after her favourite uncle.'

His comment brought a further tightening of Mrs Newson's thin lips.

Hastily, he bent over and kissed the forehead of the still-sleeping Gemma before walking round the bed and kissing the baby. The light touch woke the infant. The baby immediately screwed up his face, which quickly became as red as a cardinal's hat. Then the cardinal's hat began to scream.

'Now look what you've done,' Mrs Newson shrilled. Her thin features tightened so much Rafferty wondered she didn't cut off her own blood supply. He should be so lucky . . .

'Natural father indeed,' she snorted under her breath, but loudly enough to ensure that no one remained in ignorance of her opinion.

Reproved, Rafferty went through the *mea culpa* routine again, before, pursued by his new great-nephew's ever-more piercing screams, he rushed to the door, pausing only to blow an apologetic kiss to the now rudely awakened Gemma, relieved he had managed to make his escape before she added her complaints to those of her new son and his paternal grandmother.

Thankful to be out of range of both critical lungs and rebuking glances, once through the double doors that opened on to Elmhurst General's public car park, Rafferty paused to enjoy the warmth of the June sun on his face. He breathed in several lungfuls of air untainted by antiseptic and other, less pleasant odours before he got in the car and made for the murder scene. His relief to be making his escape courtesy of a murder victim, seemingly conjured up solely for his convenience, made him feel even guiltier.

One

Rafferty had told Llewellyn he would meet him at the murder scene. And as he parked and got out of his car close to the front entrance of Parkview Apartments, he saw the white-suited Llewellyn, who must have been watching for him, emerge from the block.

While he waited for Llewellyn to reach him, Rafferty opened the car boot, where he kept his own supply of protective clothing, and began to climb into a fresh set. As he did so, he studied the apartment's security measures: the intercom entry system, security lighting and the burglar alarm prominent on the wall. It was clear that plentiful measures had been taken to ensure the residents' peace of mind. Yet, for all the security devices, from what Llewellyn had said, one of the residents had still died a violent death in her own home.

After Llewellyn had reached Rafferty and they had exchanged greetings, Llewellyn said, 'The body's that of a Mrs Clara Mortimer. The SOCOs have arrived. We're still waiting for Dr Dally.'

Rafferty nodded. 'Have you had time to discover how many residents there are?'

Llewellyn confirmed it. 'There are ten apartments on four floors. According to the warden who supplied me with a list, most of the apartments have a single occupant.' He handed this list to Rafferty, who scrutinized it.

Of the ten apartments, five were on the third floor and presumably represented the apartments' cheapest option. The second and first floors each contained two apartments, while the ground floor housed only the warden, Rita Atkins, and what looked, from what Rafferty could see from the road, like a spacious entrance hall.

Only three of the apartments housed more than one person; married couples, seemingly. Altogether, the apartments housed thirteen people; was the dead women unlucky number thirteen? he wondered.

The majority of the single occupants were women; a fact that could be of value if this *did* turn out to be a murder investigation as Llewellyn had indicated. In Rafferty's experience women tended to take a firm interest in their neighbours and would be more likely than the male residents to notice strangers. And as solitary females without a husband's demands to take up their time, they would have ample scope for gazing from their windows.

Parkview Apartments were set in beautifully landscaped grounds with the rear parking accessed from a side service road. In front of the apartments immaculate lawns were broken up by flowerbeds; the ones on the left and right sides picked out the apartment's name in green on a red background, two of the colours in Elmhurst's town emblem. The larger centre bed contained Elmhurst's actual emblem: to the left or sinister side, on a red background, were the three seaxes or axes of Essex, which, as Llewellyn had told him, represented the reputed arms of the Saxon kings; to the right were three leaping stags on a green background to denote that Elmhurst was once a royal hunting forest. Beneath was the ancient priory with its vast landholdings depicted by a sheaf of wheat, the whole surmounted by a crown. The town's motto – 'In God We Trust' – was beneath the emblem and under this, the two dates 1204–2004, which *The Elmhurst Echo*, the local newspaper, had emblazoned on every front page since the beginning of the year, ensuring its readers were aware that Elmhurst was celebrating the eight hundredth anniversary of the granting of the town's charter by King John.

Rafferty sniffed the scented air appreciatively. With Priory Park opposite, it was certainly a beautiful and tranquil spot. Priory Way was mostly lined with expensive detached houses. Its pavements were wide and dotted with troughs containing more flowers in the red and green colours of the town's emblem. Although these looked attractive, there had been no attempt by the Council to copy Parkview Apartment's commemorative motif in the park's raised beds.

As they walked towards the entrance, Rafferty nodded to young Timothy Smales, the uniformed officer on duty at the entrance to the sheltered apartments. Thankfully, Smales seemed to have recovered from the grudge he had nursed since their last murder case. His previous sulky schoolboy demeanour had now given way to self-important zeal as he clutched his clipboard and pen.

After noting down Rafferty's name as carefully as a traffic warden set on beating his own bookings record, Smales informed him portentously, 'It's second floor front, sir – Apartment 2A.'

Rafferty nodded in acknowledgement of this information and followed Llewellyn across the threshold. He stumbled and would have fallen but for clutching at Llewellyn's arm. He regained his composure and glanced down. On top of the entrance mat proper, someone had placed what looked like a hand-made effort, a gaudy 'welcome' mat in bilious green with fussy, curly red lettering, which stuck up a good inch above the entrance. Rafferty grimaced; he'd had better welcomes.

As they climbed the stairs, Rafferty gazed round him. The carpet was thick and of good quality, the entrance hall and stairs lined with paintings, not the cheap, 'Charging Elephant' type, either.

'Nice gaff,' he commented. 'Pretty posh, considering it's sheltered housing.'

Beside him, Llewellyn said, 'It's a private block and is rather exclusive. Has a long waiting list, I understand, especially if you haven't got an influential friend on the residents' committee.'

'So the victim wasn't short of a few bob,' Rafferty remarked automatically, before he could stop himself. 'Gives us a pointer to a possible motive.'

'As you say, sir – a possible motive. But it's early days yet.'

Subtly cautioned by his sergeant, Rafferty smiled inwardly. He'd turned over a new leaf and was determined to never again race ahead of the evidence, though he hadn't shared his conversion with Llewellyn. After his last murder investigation, he wanted this conversion from old habits to come as a welcome surprise as the case unfolded.

Llewellyn confided, 'According to one of the other residents, the victim was reputed to keep quite large cash sums in her apartment.'

'Was she now? Interesting.' Rafferty was careful to say nothing further on the subject of motivational possibilities as they climbed the last step and entered the second-floor landing. There were four doors off, one apartment door on each side of the spacious hallway, with the door to a lift on their left and that of the stairwell through which they had just emerged beside it. Number 2A was on the left. The door was open with PC Lizzie Green standing to one side of it exuding her normal early-morning scent of lily of the valley talcum powder.

Rafferty suspected Lizzie Green had adopted this most maiden-aunt of perfumes as a defensive measure. He wondered when Lizzie would cotton on to the fact that most of her male colleagues found the combination of the old-fashioned aroma, her curly dark hair, bee-stung lips and voluptuous figure that even the police uniform couldn't disguise, more than a little beguiling.

Rafferty smiled good morning and gave his attention to the door lock. It was a sturdy 5-lever mortise and showed no signs of damage.

As Llewellyn had mentioned, most of the team had already arrived. Through the open door of the spacious lobby directly ahead, Rafferty could see Fraser, part of the fingerprint team and Adrian Appleby and his Scenes of Crime experts already hard at work in the living room. He stepped across the threshold and entered the lobby. A large mahogany wardrobe filled half of one wall. The others were hung with more pictures and a large, ornately framed mirror.

Seven years' bad luck for someone, he thought automatically, as he saw the shattered shards of glass littering the pale-green carpet. Then he thought again of the victim, whose bad luck encompassed all eternity and his guilty feelings came back in full measure.

The body was in the living room. As, currently, Lance Edwards was hovering over it with his video camera, Rafferty addressed his attention to the rest of the scene.

The living room was large, around twenty feet by twenty-five, richly furnished in an old-fashioned style, with more heavy mahogany furniture and lots of old ladies' knick-knacks and ornaments, not cheap gimcrack items, either. All were tasteful in a restrained way; delicate cream-coloured figurines of ballerinas performed their elegant, eternal dance beside coy Edwardian maidens of downcast demeanour.

The victim had a huge collection of long-playing records; the covers that he could see were mostly classical and neatly shelved in their sleeves. The many books lining the walls also indicated the victim had been a woman of cultured interests – the ballet featured strongly as well as opera, history and travel.

The room didn't appear to have been ransacked at all. Rafferty concluded that the intruder had panicked after discovering he had a dead body on his hands.

He took a few more minutes to study the rest of the room. He noted the pile of around half a dozen unopened envelopes on the mantelpiece; they looked like birthday cards. Saved for when? Surely not today? he wondered.

But as he studied the postmark on the top envelope and saw it had been posted with a first-class stamp locally the previous morning, he realized his guess must be correct. It made the murder more poignant and his guilty feelings even more potent.

He recalled Llewellyn's remark that the dead old lady was reputed to keep money in her apartment and, briefly, he wondered why the elderly should persist with such a naive practice in today's crime-ridden world. How many stories about violent burglary did the elderly members of society need to read before they adopted more sensible measures?

Beside him, Llewellyn followed his gaze to the pile of birthday card envelopes. He murmured, 'Perhaps her killer, like the Greeks, came bearing gifts as an excuse to gain entrance?'

'The fates are unlikely to be that kind,' Rafferty said. 'It would suit me if we could confine our suspect list to the family member or friend whose card *isn't* still here. But I don't imagine the cards will fall our way.'

He turned away from the pile of cards whose recipient would now never open them and studied the rest of the room. There was a panic button close to the small side table next to where Clara Mortimer lay. Had she not had time to press it? he wondered. Or had fear frozen her mind and limbs?

The table held a couple of framed photographs. One, in age-faded sepia, was of a young man in an RAF uniform – a brother, perhaps? If so, he would, hopefully, still be alive and would be able to tell them something of the dead woman's life, routine and acquaintances.

The second photograph was a much more recent snap. It showed a colourful seaside scene – in the forefront a young boy smiled with the gap-toothed charm of a seven-year-old.

Rafferty guessed that the broadly smiling middle-aged female behind the boy was the younger version of the dead woman.

He looked round the rest of the room, but there were no other photographs. Such a paucity of photographs indicated that either Clara Mortimer had little in the way of family or that she had been remarkably unsentimental – unusual in a woman who Llewellyn had told him must be in her late sixties or early seventies.

Out of keeping with the quiet elegance of the remainder, the décor struck a jarring note. Two walls had recently been painted – badly, with runs and missing patches clearly visible – a bright, peacock blue that argued with the muted green colour scheme of the rest.

He checked the windows and noted that, like the door, none of them showed signs of having been tampered with.

At last, as Lance Edwards moved away from the victim, Rafferty walked over to the body.

Clara Mortimer lay sprawled on her back. Her skirt had rucked up as she fell, exposing sensible white knickers and skinny old lady's thighs: the ultimate indignity of death. The right side of her forehead was stoved in. The blow had crushed one eye in its socket; the other stared pitifully up at him, its pale-grey iris already fading. Rafferty thought he could read a plea for help in the sightless eye as it gazed at him.

Avoiding again meeting that beseeching orb whose owner was now beyond anyone's help, he hunkered down beside the body and checked for other injuries. None was evident, not even defence injuries to her hands, though clearly she had been attacked from the front. Along with her failure to use the conveniently positioned panic button to summon aid, it was another pointer to her having been frozen with fright and unable to defend herself.

From her elegantly styled and now bloodied white hair, gathered in a French plait at the back of her head, to the expensive cashmere jumper and dainty – real? – pearls in her ears, to the low-heeled leather shoes rather than the more common bedroom slippers of early-morning, Clara Mortimer appeared far from the usual run of sad and vulnerable elderly ladies they saw at scenes of violent death.

Rafferty stood up and turned to Llewellyn. 'Let's go and have a look round the rest of the apartment. Then I want a word with the warden, Mrs Atkins. She should be able to let us have details of Mrs Mortimer's family.' He tapped the list Llewellyn had given him. 'The residents will all have to be questioned as a matter of priority.'

Clara Mortimer's apartment had two spacious bedrooms off the lobby, both with double beds, though the bed in the second bedroom wasn't made up and the room had an entirely unlived-in appearance.

Rafferty, expecting to find more family photographs in Clara Mortimer's bedroom, was surprised and saddened when they found none. He immediately pictured his ma's living room with its walls crammed with family photographs and felt that, for all her obvious riches, the dead woman cut as pitiful and lonely a figure as more impoverished elderly and lone-living victims of crime.

There was no sign that anyone else lived in the apartment; there were none of the welcoming touches usual in a guest room. Old ladies' clothes in expensive fabrics, summer silks and winter cashmere, were the only clothes in the cavernous mahogany wardrobes. He presumed Mrs Mortimer's husband must be dead and found himself hoping – and not just for the sake of the murder investigation – that the victim hadn't been as all alone in the world as she appeared to be.

There was one way to find out and he said to Llewellyn, 'Let's go and speak to the warden.'

They left the rest of the team to get on with their work and went back to the ground floor, where, according to the residents' list, the warden had a small apartment. He followed Llewellyn through a door to the rear of the entrance hall. It led to a short, wholly enclosed and dimly lit corridor. It smelt musty. The opulence of the rest of the block ended abruptly. Here there was no expensive carpet or original artwork. In their place were cheap vinyl and bare walls, the warden's apartment seemingly squeezed in as an afterthought.

Although the morning was now well advanced, Rita Atkins, a small, slight woman, answered their knock in a none-too-clean woollen dressing gown in an unflattering shade of beige. As she peered up at them in the enveloping gloom, her expression appeared glazed. And as she stood aside to let them in, Rafferty caught a whiff of whisky. So it wasn't only the shock of sudden, violent death that had caused the glazed eyes. He could hardly blame such a tiny, vulnerable woman for taking a nip of something restorative in the circumstances. When he thought of Clara Mortimer's smashed-in eye and the other one, staring up at him, Rafferty felt he could do with a restorative nip of something himself. But as Dr Sam Dally, who could always be relied upon to supply such liquid refreshment, had yet to arrive, Rafferty had perforce to do without.

Rita Atkins's apartment seemed as tiny as the exterior had indicated. As she led them the short step from her apartment's front door to her living room, he took in the rest. A single, small bedroom led off the two-yard-square hallway. An overflowing wardrobe and a single bed took up all the floor space. Beside it was a bathroom that looked to have dimensions no bigger than a large broom cupboard. A tiny kitchen was immediately off to the left of the front door. It looked out on the covered dustbin enclosure. Rita Atkins's living room had a musty, uncared-for air and shared the kitchen's unattractive outlook.

In total contrast to the second-floor apartment of Clara Mortimer, here were family photographs by the score, but he saw no sign of any interest in music or books. The only reading matter was a scattering of tabloid newspapers, a television guide with the day's viewing already marked and women's magazines of the celebrity-worshipping variety. These battled for space on the small coffee table with TV and video zappers, cigarettes, an overflowing ashtray and a veritable Highland Clan of miniatures of Scotch whisky.

Mrs Atkins must have observed Rafferty's interest in the latter for, perhaps in order to staunch any suspicion that she was into solitary morning drinking, she was quick to explain them away.

'The apartment residents bring them back for me from their various exotic holidays; probably bought on the plane home as last-minute gifts for "Poor Rita", who never goes anywhere.'

Although she laughed and tried to make a joke of it, Rafferty caught a hint of resentment in her voice. He couldn't really blame her if she should dislike being patronized in return for miniatures of the least expensive whisky on the market, especially as it didn't seem likely that Rita Atkins would be in a position to frequently jet off to exotic climes.

He felt a brief urge to ask her if she could spare him one or two of the full miniatures; thankfully the urge passed.

Although she had been quick to explain that she hadn't bought the bottles herself, Rafferty noted that, although the full ones were artfully placed round the outside as if to act as a shield, most of the collection of twenty or so were empty. He wondered why she kept them. But a quick glance around the living room told him that Rita Atkins was a collector of the trifles that other people threw away; empty miniatures, curling postcards, even personally addressed junk mail seemed to be treasured. The hoarding of the latter indicated that Rita Atkins received little in the way of personal mail.

Invited to sit down, he and Llewellyn perched companionably on a scarred, red leatherette two-seater settee and waited for Rita Atkins to squeeze past and settle on the matching armchair set at right angles to the settee before he asked her if she could provide him with a list of Clara Mortimer's known visitors.

She fetched a writing pad and pen from the top of the TV cupboard and jotted down some names. It didn't take long. As Mrs Atkins kept up a running commentary while she jotted down the names, they learned that the victim's only visitors had been her daughter, Jane Ogilvie, Darryl somebody – surname unknown, the daughter's current live-in boyfriend, and a woman, Mary Soames, who, as Rita Atkins explained, until Clara Mortimer's recent move to the sheltered apartments, had been a close neighbour and long-term friend of the victim.

'Nice woman. Always has a friendly word,' she remarked.

Unlike *whom*? Rafferty wondered; the late Clara Mortimer, perhaps? Though if Mrs Atkins had considered bringing any grudge against Mrs Mortimer to its ultimate conclusion, Rafferty couldn't see the tiny, bird-like Rita Atkins in the role of murderer, not least because she was unlikely to instil frozen panic in anyone, certainly not the much taller and stronger-looking Mrs Mortimer.

A few minutes' questioning of Rita Atkins elicited the information that Clara Mortimer had been more or less estranged from her family.

'They rarely visited,' Rita Atkins was quick to confide, as though anxious for them to know that for all her evident wealth, Clara Mortimer didn't share *her* rich endowment of family ties. 'All the other residents noticed and remarked on it.'

Rita Atkins's skin, which Rafferty guessed would normally be as pallid and washed out as her dressing gown, this morning bore mottled red patches, though whether these were caused by nerves or drink, he had no idea.

'Her daughter, Jane Ogilvie – or whatever she's calling herself this week – was only an occasional visitor. Even when she turned up, she never stayed for long. Her boyfriend – Darryl, I think he's called – he's younger than her – also turned up a few times lately, and made a half-hearted attempt at decorating for Mrs Mortimer. Trying to curry favour, I took it. But it didn't last long.'

That explained the half-finished and amateurishly applied blue paint on Mrs Mortimer's living-room walls, which he had already noted. Perhaps, as Mrs Atkins said, the half-done decorating had been started in an attempt to curry favour. It hadn't worked, as Rita Atkins explained.

'Mrs Mortimer sent him packing. She accused him of stealing from her. I heard them arguing about it on the landing outside her flat. Going at it hammer and tongs, they were, with him ranting about her being ungrateful.'

Rafferty glanced at Llewellyn. 'When was this?' he asked the warden.

She frowned. 'It must be a week ago now. I haven't seen him or Jane since. Though as I said, Jane wasn't what you'd call a regular visitor. Sometimes weeks would go by between visits.'

'Do you know where Mrs Mortimer's daughter lives?' Llewellyn put in. 'You said her surname's Ogilvie?'

The warden pulled a face. 'I know she lives in Mercer's Lane; it's off the High Street, near the East Hill end. Go up Eastchepe and it's the first road on the right. Jane lives at number twelve, I think. But as for her name . . . Maybe she's calling herself Ogilvie again, or maybe she's adopted another name. Your guess as to what it might be this week is as good as mine. She has a habit of calling herself by the name of her latest live-in boyfriend,' she explained with an accompanying sniff. 'I got the impression there's been quite a succession of them. I understand that not one of her children has the same surname – she had three children last time Mrs Mortimer mentioned them; a bit of a Heinz 57

20

varieties they are, too. I've seen them out together a couple of times, though I've never seen any of them visiting Mrs Mortimer since she moved here.

'Jane Ogilvie doesn't bother to bring them to see her mother. But then, as I said, she rarely troubled to visit her mother herself. It must have been upsetting for poor Mrs Mortimer, though she never talked about it. Too proud to be willing to acknowledge how far her family had fallen, I suppose.'

Rafferty and Llewellyn exchanged another glance at this. Rafferty wondered how Mrs Mortimer had felt to be the recipient of pity from Rita Atkins. Clara Mortimer and her daughter sounded as if they must have been total opposites. Even in death Mrs Mortimer had looked well-groomed and fastidious. If she was as old-fashioned as her furniture and other possessions indicated and her daughter was as promiscuous as she sounded it was no wonder they were estranged.

Rafferty was pleased to learn about Mary Soames, the victim's previous neighbour. It sounded as if she must have known Clara Mortimer for some years, so should have valuable information to share. Although Rita Atkins didn't know her address, she was able to tell them Mrs Soames lived in a big house a bit outside the southern outskirts of Elmhurst, so shouldn't be too difficult to track down.

Rafferty asked her to add the names of those among the other residents that she knew to have been on visiting terms with Clara Mortimer.

Mrs Atkins looked doubtful, but after some thought added another three names, those of a married couple, the Toombes and the other newcomer to the block, Hal Oliver.

'I think he might have been sweet on her,' Rita Atkins confided. 'I saw him knock on her door once, shortly after he moved in, carrying a big bunch of roses. They were red, too.' She sounded bemused by this and not a little envious.

But if Rita Atkins envied Clara Mortimer her gentleman caller, Rafferty, for one, was pleased to hear that the solitary

Clara Mortimer had an admirer. He took the list the warden had compiled and thanked her.

'There might have been other visitors,' Mrs Atkins told them. She immediately added, in a sharp tone, as if worried they might think she did so in order to fill her own empty existence, 'I don't keep a guard on the door to watch all the comings and goings, so the names I gave you are the only ones I know for certain.'

'That's fine. You've been very helpful,' Rafferty assured her. He consulted his hastily scribbled notes. 'I understand a Miss Amelia Frobisher found the body?'

For some reason this comment caused Rita Atkins's lips to purse. She gave a stiff nod.

'Miss Frobisher's in Apartment 2B?' Rafferty questioned.

Rita Atkins nodded again. 'It's across the corridor from Mrs Mortimer's apartment, though I doubt Amelia Frobisher will be able to tell you much about Clara's life. They didn't speak. Not lately, anyway.'

'Really? Do you know why that was?'

As he had intended, the question acted as a spur for Rita to show off her knowledge.

'Several things spring to mind.' She smiled and displayed small, pointed teeth. They were as stained and dingy as her dressing gown. 'For one thing, Amelia Frobisher accused Mrs Mortimer of stealing Freddie Talbot, her gentleman friend. She hadn't, of course, as Clara Mortimer made clear. It was quite a longstanding relationship until Mrs Mortimer moved here. Then, Amelia's gentleman friend cooled and switched his attentions to Mrs Mortimer with what Amelia must have felt was an insulting alacrity. To add insult to injury, Mrs Mortimer not only made plain that she wasn't interested in Fancy Freddie as I call him, she rejected him publicly in the entrance foyer. It must have been about a month ago. I was dusting the pictures there. I can still remember her exact words. She said, "For goodness sake, you sad man. Go back to Amelia Frobisher. She might be grateful for your attentions, *I'm not.*'"

Humiliating for Talbot, thought Rafferty, especially when the put down had obviously been witnessed by the warden.

'Amelia Frobisher, as the longest resident, has always taken it upon herself to act the grande dame hostess to new residents.' With another sniff, Rita Atkins went on. 'She's always organizing outings and pushing the other residents to sign up for them. I suspect she must get a discount on the tickets and pocket the difference. She even organizes birthday teas for the other residents in her apartment as if she and they were proper family. Clara Mortimer would have none of it. She had rebuffed her several times. Amelia resented her for it. I heard her call Clara "standoffish" to her face once. Clara just cut her dead. Clara received no more invitations after Freddie Talbot, Amelia's beau, transferred his affections, particularly as he failed to do what Clara had suggested and go back to Amelia. Not that she would have taken him back. Amelia's too full of pride and vanity to so humiliate herself.'

'I see.' Whether Clara Mortimer had had good reason to have a down on Amelia Frobisher, it was clear, from the relish with which she related the gossip, that Rita Atkins felt she owed Amelia Frobisher a spiteful thrust or three.

Beside him, Llewellyn asked, 'Did you go on these outings, Mrs Atkins?'

'Me? No.' Her lips turned down. 'I'm only the warden of the block. I was never invited. I didn't get a birthday tea, either. Not that I wanted them any more than Mrs Mortimer. But, as I said, Amelia Frobisher likes to give herself airs. And grande dames don't socialize below their own pecking order.'

Nice to get on with the neighbours, Rafferty thought, as he digested the apartments' tittle-tattle. And for all Amelia Frobisher's attempts to play Happy Families with the other residents – attempts that struck Rafferty as more indicative of Miss Frobisher's own loneliness than grande dame tendencies – she seemed to have conjured up more resentment than true family feeling.

'Tell me,' he said. 'As warden, you must spend more time in the entrance lobby than the other residents. Have you seen any strangers hanging about lately?'

She shook her head. 'None, apart from the occasional group of yobs who used to hang about the park. But I haven't even seen any of them lately.' She gave a down-turned smile and told him slyly, 'When the rich shout, the police tend to come running. The yobs certainly seem to have got the message. I suppose they've found somewhere else to make a nuisance of themselves now.'

Rafferty made no attempt to defend his colleagues. It was a fact of life that those who shouted loudest invariably got the most attention, whether it was the police who were being shouted at or local bigwigs. Certainly, he couldn't imagine his superintendent, Long Pockets Bradley, permitting his officers to be neglectful of those of wealth and influence.

'Did you hear any odd noises this morning?'

'No, not this morning.'

As she said this, an ugly flush crept up Rita Atkins's neck and blended with the red patches still adorning her cheeks. It gave her an unhealthy raddled look. Worried that this sudden deeper flushing might indicate the deliberate concealment of evidence, Rafferty questioned her more sharply.

'You're sure you didn't see or hear anything? Anything at all?'

'No. I told you I didn't. As a matter of fact, I woke late this morning as I slept through my alarm.'

Doubtless, the alcohol she had downed the night before had been the cause, thought Rafferty, who had himself suffered a few similar unscheduled lie-ins.

'To return to something you said earlier,' Llewellyn broke in. 'I believe you said there were several things that had caused resentments between Miss Frobisher and Mrs Mortimer?'

Rita Atkins nodded with every appearance of relief at getting off a subject that clearly embarrassed her.

'What were the other things?'

Rita gave Llewellyn another smile, one even wider than before.

Rafferty guessed that, notwithstanding Clara Mortimer's violent death, supplying answers to their questions about the late Mrs Mortimer and who might have reason to bear a grudge against her had quite made her morning.

'You want to ask Amelia Frobisher about the mat,' she said.

As Rafferty and Llewellyn exchanged another bemused glance, she explained. 'The garish welcome mat at the entrance was another cause for resentment. Amelia made it, but Clara Mortimer complained to me about it. Naturally, I had words with Miss Frobisher.'

Rafferty gained the distinct impression that Rita Atkins had thoroughly enjoyed these 'words'. She must have considered it the downtrodden's revenge.

'I told Amelia Frobisher that the mat had to go. Apart from contravening one of the covenants governing the block, it's a danger to life and limb.'

Having tripped over it himself, Rafferty found himself nodding agreement. 'So why is it still there?' he asked.

'Because Amelia Frobisher doesn't take kindly to being told what to do, certainly not by me. We've had a regular tussle about it since. Every time I remove it, she puts it back. I'd burn the wretched thing if I didn't think she'd make another one even more hideous.'

'I see.' Rafferty stood up. 'Thanks for your help, Mrs Atkins. We may need to speak to you again,' he told her as he and Llewellyn made for the door, eager to escape the warden's musty little cell.

Her tone now surly, with discontent creeping in at the

edges, she told them abruptly, 'You know where to find me.'

'Wonder what's made her so prickly?' Rafferty mused as Rita Atkins closed her apartment door behind them. But as they opened the door leading to the large, airy and sweet-smelling entrance hall, the contrast hit him and he gained a sudden insight in to how Rita Atkins must feel. Because, if, like Rita Atkins as she went about her cleaning duties, he had to walk through the door that separated her dim and musty den from the magic kingdom, he could imagine people would soon have reason to think he had as many prickles as a thorny hedge.

Llewellyn, of course, provided a logical answer to his musing.

'Apart from the obvious fact that she had a deep resentment towards Miss Frobisher and her grande dame ways, I presume it was part of Mrs Atkins's job to keep a check on the welfare of the residents. Maybe she thought, by finding the body, Miss Frobisher had usurped her role. It's often the case that people with limited responsibilities become territorial about those duties.'

Rafferty nodded at this. Curious to see what Amelia Frobisher had to say for herself, he turned towards the stairs. However, before he had advanced two steps, Dr Sam Dally arrived with his usual bustle.

As Rafferty escorted him to the victim's apartment, he filled him in on what they had so far learned.

'It's clear to me the way your mind's working, Rafferty,' Dally remarked. 'You think the old lady let in someone she knew and was then knocked on the head and robbed by this person.'

'Not necessarily,' Rafferty protested, sensitive about his reputation for leaping to conclusions early in a case. Of course, Sam, like Llewellyn, was unaware that he'd sworn off such behaviour. 'We don't know yet if any money or valuables are missing, though as the victim seemed to have kept herself to herself and was apparently all but estranged from her family, I don't know how we can be sure either way. Certainly, the apartment doesn't *look* as though it's been ransacked, though the intruder might easily have panicked when he realized he'd killed her, before he had a chance to do so.'

They reached Clara Mortimer's apartment. With several huffs and puffs, the generously proportioned Sam Dally lowered himself to his plump knees beside the body and began his examination.

Rafferty, with so much to think about at the busy start of another murder inquiry, had forgotten about the victim's pitifully staring, undamaged eye. Now, he tersely demanded of Lance Edwards, the photographer, if he had finished taking pictures of the body. When Lance nodded, Rafferty suggested Dally shut the staring orb.

'Giving you the evil eye, is she?' Dally asked as his fat fingers drew the lid down.

'When do you reckon it happened?' Rafferty asked a few minutes later when Dally had tested the temperature of the room and done his calculations.

'I'd say no more than three hours ago. The undamaged eye's only beginning to go cloudy and the lividity isn't yet complete. Rigor's only evident in the eyelids and jaw so far. All indications point to a timescale of no more than three hours ago, possibly less.'

It was now just after ten in the morning; that would put her death at no earlier than 7.00 a.m. Clara Mortimer must have been an early-riser to be up, dressed and ready for the day at such an hour – unless she had been expecting an early visitor . . . ?

Given her seeming preference for a solitary existence, that seemed unlikely, but the possibility couldn't be discounted.

'What do you think the assailant used for a weapon?'

'Some blunt instrument,' Dally replied. 'A cosh or something similar.'

Rafferty nodded. As it struck him as unlikely that Clara Mortimer would own a cosh, it seemed probable that her murderer had brought the weapon with him and although they had yet to make a thorough search of the apartment, it seemed equally likely that the murderer had taken the weapon away with him.

Once Dally had departed and the Coroner's Officer had given permission for the removal of the body to the mortuary, Rafferty headed across the landing to Amelia Frobisher's apartment. After Rita Atkins's revelations about the love-lorn 'Fancy' Freddie Talbot, he was curious to see this second, scorned, female member of the ageing love triangle for himself.

Two

Amelia Frobisher's door opened immediately to their knock. Rafferty wondered if she had been waiting behind it with her eye glued to the spy hole.

Perhaps aware that her response to their knock might imply an unseemly morbid curiosity, after Rafferty had introduced Llewellyn and himself, Amelia Frobisher covered her haste by adopting the superior air of one to whom nosiness was foreign. And although only around five feet six and disadvantaged by her lack of stature, this didn't stop her trying to look down her long nose at them in true grande dame style.

After studying them for some moments through popping, pale-blue eyes that indicated some thyroid problem, her inquisitiveness about her neighbour's murder overcame any inclination to gentile aloofness and she ushered them inside with a speed that indicated her curiosity could abide no more delays.

Miss Frobisher's apartment – like Miss Frobisher herself – was as different again from Clara Mortimer's and Rita Atkins's as it was possible to be. The décor of the apartment tended to the fussy, as did the clothes style of Miss Frobisher. Perhaps she shared the late Duchess of Windsor's belief that you could never be too rich or too thin, for Amelia Frobisher was thin to the point of emaciation. Her chosen outfit of frilly, three-quarter-sleeved blouse and A-line skirt with another frill adorning its hem, only served to emphasize her stick-like figure.

Rafferty, after hearing about the organizing, rather bossy-sounding Miss Frobisher, had expected her to be more physically imposing.

Most of Amelia Frobisher's living room was taken up by three fat pink sofas, each of which had more frills than the Rafferty family's heirloom baptismal gown. The blinds were those flouncy things that reminded Rafferty of old-fashioned women's tennis bloomers. As he looked at them, in his head, he could hear his ma's voice scorn them as dust-gatherers.

Amelia Frobisher shared one interior design preference with Rita Atkins. Photographs overflowed every surface. Invitations to weddings, christenings and birthday parties jostled for space on the mantelpiece. For all that she was an elderly spinster, it looked as though Amelia Frobisher enjoyed a rich and full life in the bosom of her family.

It was only as Rafferty got closer and studied them that he saw each of the invitations was penned by a remarkably similar hand. It occurred to him that Miss Frobisher had written them to herself in order to impress the other residents with the esteem in which she was held in her family.

From over his shoulder, Miss Frobisher's voice chilled the room by several degrees as she asked – nay, *insisted*, he take a seat. Her tone was frosty with annoyance as though – even though the invitations were displayed for the world to see – she felt his examination of such private things showed bad manners.

He felt her popping eyes bore into his back and he looked hastily away from the array of cards in case she guessed his suspicion and he invited non-cooperation so early in the case.

But he needn't have worried; it seemed Amelia Frobisher was one of those people who lived on the surface of life and who only saw what they chose to see. Once he had done her bidding and taken a seat, she gave him a complacent smile that revealed dentures overlarge for her gaunt face.

Settled opposite the better-mannered Llewellyn, in an

armchair upholstered in more fussy flounces, she nodded towards all the photographs and invitations and in a voice that managed to be gushing and condescending at the same time, she said, 'Quite a crew, wouldn't you say, Inspector? I often used to feel sorry for poor, dear Clara, seeing so little of her family. So sad.'

This was the second resident of the sheltered block to express pity for Clara Mortimer. Again, Rafferty wondered how Mrs Mortimer had felt to be the recipient of such sentiments.

'We're just trying to establish the late Mrs Mortimer's background,' he said.

Amelia Frobisher sat up even straighter, if that was possible, her head tilted at an angle as she waited for him to continue.

'I understand from the warden that Mrs Mortimer had a daughter?'

Miss Frobisher nodded and smoothed her pepper-and-salt bun of hair even though it had no need of smoothing as it was held firmly in place by what Rafferty thought was called a snood.

'Though you'd never know from Clara that she had a daughter; I only learned of this daughter's existence when she turned up here one day last week trailing some young man who strutted about as though he owned the place. Although he was much younger, I gained the distinct impression he was some kind of boyfriend. He had bleached hair and jeans that were so tight they verged on the obscene.'

With a few, tiny alterations to her features – a flare of a nostril here and a downturn to a lip there – Amelia Frobisher managed to convey her low opinion of Darryl No-name.

Rafferty was amused to note that her low opinion of Darryl hadn't stopped her taking what sounded like a more than passing glance at Darryl's tightly bejeaned nether regions. He thought he detected a frisson of regret, too, that a young man of such cocky confidence had never trailed after *her*.

Even 'Fancy' Freddie Talbot, he of the wandering eye, had proved less than accommodating in the trailing department, if what Rita Atkins had told them was true.

'He caused a scene,' she told them.

From her disapproving tone, Rafferty guessed that, to her, this was one of the great social solecisms.

Her features rearranged themselves into less judgemental lines though she was unable to conceal the gratification in her voice as she added, 'I must say, I was astonished to discover that Clara's daughter should be such an unkempt creature. No wonder Clara never spoke of her.' Her demure air retreated a little under her satisfaction at this. 'I think Clara must have been ashamed of her.'

Unsurprising, Rafferty thought, if what the warden had told him about the daughter was true. 'You found Mrs Mortimer's body, I understand?'

'Yes, I'd just been down to rescue my mat and . . .' Amelia Frobisher's lips compressed as if she had just realized she had let slip something she would rather have kept to herself. Then the thin lips parted to add – in a throwaway air that more or less said, 'What else can you expect from the hired help?' – 'But I imagine Rita Atkins has already told you all about that.'

Rafferty nodded. 'Mrs Atkins did mention something of the sort. I understand that Mrs Mortimer complained to her about it.'

'It was a big fuss over nothing,' she retorted. 'I don't know what Rita Atkins has been saying to you, Inspector, but knowing Rita, she'll have made it sound as if the apartments were engulfed in some kind of civil war. It was only a mat, for goodness sake, scarcely a worthy cause for bringing out the big battalions.'

'So Mrs Mortimer's complaint caused no enmity between you?'

'*Enmity?*' she repeated sharply. 'Certainly not. What a ridiculous idea.' With a note of condescension cooling her

voice, she remarked, 'Poor Rita longs for a little colour in her drab drudge's life, Inspector. You noticed those appalling "celebrity" magazines that she reads littering her living room?'

Rafferty gave a brief nod of acknowledgement.

'Not to put too fine a point on it, Rita Atkins has a tendency to dramatize daily life. And if it's not dramatic enough for her, she improves on it. She exists more in a make-believe world than in reality. I understand that in the eighteen months she's been warden here, she's worn out two video recorders and a – a DVD, would it be?'

Rafferty nodded. He could see no sign of a TV, video or DVD in Amelia Frobisher's living room, although a whole shop-full of electrical gadgets could, doubtless, have found concealment beneath the many frills and flounces. He could only suppose their non-existence went to support the myth that, with her busy social life amongst her loving family, she wouldn't have time for such frivolities – although the fact that she had leisure enough to make a time-consuming and ugly mat for the entrance rather gave the lie to this.

Rafferty was about to mention the fickle Freddie Talbot when, as if suspecting that Rita Atkins would have taken pleasure in revealing Talbot's betrayal, Amelia Frobisher brought the subject up herself. She succeeded in making light of it.

'I used to have a gentleman acquaintance, a Mr Frederick Talbot. He was only a friend, nothing more. It was a friendship of habit rather than one of depth. I was rather relieved to have an excuse to cut him off when he made a fool of himself with Clara Mortimer. As I told him, I expect my friends to have a certain dignity, especially when they're old enough to have learned how to behave. He'd embarrassed me by his foolish importuning of Clara.'

Her embarrassment was unlikely to have been reduced when she learned this importuning had been witnessed by Rita Atkins. Rafferty had already concluded that social

embarrassment would be top of Amelia Frobisher's list of intolerable behaviour in others.

The importunate and humiliated Freddie Talbot would have to be checked out; it wasn't only *women* scorned who reacted with violence and Freddie Talbot had been scorned twice over – once by Mrs Mortimer and then by the betrayed and aggrieved Amelia Frobisher. With difficulty, he persuaded Miss Frobisher to supply them with his address and phone number.

After he had soothed her ruffled flounces at this indignity, she calmed down sufficiently to return to what she had been talking about previously.

'I might have known that the little differences Clara Mortimer and I had over the mat and Freddy Talbot would be seized on by Rita and blown out of proportion. They were both fusses over trifles' – thus was Freddie Talbot's defection dismissed. 'As for the mat – I made it – Clara took exception to it being in the public area of the apartments and complained to Rita Atkins.' Miss Frobisher gave a weary sigh for the problems brought by the serving classes and added, 'Mrs Atkins and I have a particularly difficult relationship, Inspector. She's a woman of limited social skills and has an unfortunate tendency to loudness and vulgarity. She's also an inveterate gossip, as I'm sure you discovered for yourself.'

Miss Frobisher, no slouch in the gossip stakes herself, sat back, apparently well pleased with her character assassination.

'Anyway, unsurprisingly, Rita Atkins chose to take Clara's side. She told me it was against the apartments' covenant for residents to place personal items in shared areas and removed my mat. Put it out with the rubbish if you please. Her highhandedness annoyed me, I admit.' Amelia Frobisher's thin bosom arched bantam-like, then subsided. 'But it was *Mrs Atkins* I was annoyed with rather than Clara.

'Besides –' something resembling a laugh escaped from

Amelia Frobisher's mousetrap mouth – 'I knew from her attendance at the residents' committee meetings that Clara could be something of a stickler for rules and regulations, so I was half expecting her to speak to the warden about it. Rita Atkins makes a habit of removing my mat and I, as regularly, put it back.'

This time the laugh was more of a girlish giggle struggling and failing to be coy. Issuing, as it did from the throat of the repressive Miss Frobisher, it brought a shiver to Rafferty's spine. Instinctively, he shrank back and was tightly embraced by the fat sofa, which wasn't nearly as soft as it looked, while Miss Frobisher continued with her girlish confidences.

'It's become quite a little game between us,' she went on, 'and at least it gives Rita a reason to get up at a respectable hour. I was intending to rescue my mat again this morning, when I noticed Clara's apartment door wasn't shut properly – it's one of those awkward doors and doesn't close if not pulled firmly by the door handle. Clara had the knack for it, though not everyone did. Anyway, I suppose Mrs Atkins got her wish because by the time I thought about the mat, it was too late to rescue it. Today's the day the rubbish is collected,' she explained.

Since he had tripped over it, it was clear that the late-sleeping warden had this morning failed to remove the offending mat.

He was turning in to Mr Popularity today, Rafferty thought. Not only had he already improved Rita Atkins's day, he suspected, as he opened his mouth to tell Amelia Frobisher that her mat was safe and still in place, that he was about to do the same for her. He could only pray she resisted any further attempts at coy flirtation when he told her the good news.

She flushed up, pink as her three fat settees when he told her and gave Rafferty a beam of approval such as he rarely received. But, to forestall anything further in the way of gratitude from Amelia Frobisher, he was quick to jump in.

'If we could just get back to more important matters – what time was it that you found Mrs Mortimer's body?'

'It was eight o'clock. I remember Clara's beautiful mantel clock chimed the hour as I knocked and called her name. It was such a shock to find her like that, all bloodied and with her clothes in disarray.' Amelia Frobisher put a fluttering hand to her thin bosom. 'I thought this was a safe block. I can't understand how the man who attacked her can have got in. I don't believe any of the residents would be so careless of our security as to buzz strangers in. We're quite a little family here, you see, and we look out for one another.'

What family was that? Rafferty wondered. The Borgias? Their ruthless way of dispatching any who would thwart the family ambitions seemed to him to have something of an echo in this 'family', given the violence with which Clara Mortimer had been dispatched.

In spite of his no doubt fanciful comparison, Rafferty had noticed a fleeting bleakness in Miss Frobisher's eyes when she spoke of being a 'family' and he wondered – in spite of the plentiful and strategically placed 'invitations' – if her own family weren't quite as welcoming as the carefully gathered collection of party invitations implied. It would explain her determination to create a second family amongst her fellow residents even if this desire seemed to bring with it more resentment and ill feeling than was usual in half a dozen such ill-assorted 'families'.

As if determined to outface him and the possibility that he had discovered the shameful secret that her blood kin, rather than issuing invitations to assorted family knees-ups, actually kept her at arm's length, when she spoke again, Amelia Frobisher's voice had acquired a determined jollity.

'As I said, we're quite a little family here. We have our birthday teas and our regular outings to the local theatre, though generally only to matinees, as some of my fellow residents don't care to be out after dark. Occasionally, we even take a trip to one of the West End theatres. We have a charabanc to pick us up and bring us back. It's all most wonderful fun.'

Llewellyn, who, until now, had sat unobtrusively taking notes, put a stop to the telling of these jolly japes with a pertinent question to which they already had the answer. 'And did Mrs Mortimer join you on these outings?'

Rafferty struggled out of the grip of the sofa, curious to see how Miss Frobisher handled the humiliating revelation of her rebuff at Clara Mortimer's hands.

Amelia Frobisher, given Rita Atkins's previous failures at discretion and 'family' solidarity in the face of hostile, questioning outsiders, had apparently decided she had no choice but to admit that she had been rebuffed. But it was clear from the strained laugh and narrowed, unforgiving gaze, that Rita's little rebellion that necessitated such an admission, would not be lightly forgotten.

'No. Regretfully, Clara was inclined to be a little anti-social. It was such a shame, I thought, that she seemed to want to hide herself away in her apartment rather than make friends with her fellow residents, so I – perhaps foolishly in hindsight – persisted with my invitations. I don't like to speak ill of the dead, but really, her manner was quite ungracious. *Not* the way I was taught was the polite way to turn down invitations.'

With her faintly regretful air, Amelia Frobisher seemed to be trying to make light of the matter. But Rafferty had no difficulty catching the underlying implication that Clara Mortimer, with her ungracious manners, her slovenly daughter and the daughter's strutting toy boy wasn't quite the lady she had put herself forward as being.

Rafferty preferred to give the late Mrs Mortimer the benefit of any lingering doubt. He could believe that politeness would prove but a frail defence against the assault of an Amelia Frobisher determined to fill the seats of the hired charabanc to capacity.

'As the resident with the longest tenure, I feel it's my duty to welcome newcomers, especially those, like Clara Mortimer, who live alone, even when, like Clara Mortimer, they rebuff my overtures.'

Obviously keen that they should share her mystified dismay at Clara Mortimer's discourteous rebuff to her friendly overtures, she proceeded to give the other, apparently more biddable, residents a metaphorical pat on the head as though to display how very unreasonable the late Mrs Mortimer had been.

'All of the other residents appreciate and value my friendship and that I spend my limited free time in arranging theatre trips and so on for them. They're grateful to have a willing listening ear when they want to talk about their children and grandchildren. Really, I think that without my adoption of them, most would be as isolated and alone as Clara Mortimer. Although I share Clara's more cultured tastes for the opera and the ballet, I defer to the majority preference, so we mostly go to popular shows and musicals. I suppose, like myself, Clara developed a taste for high art in her youth. I understand hers was quite a privileged one.'

Another reason for Amelia Frobisher to resent her, Rafferty guessed. It was clear that Amelia considered herself the 'Queen Bee' of Parkview Apartments. She wouldn't have relished the rebuff from a woman of equal or maybe even higher social and family status.

Perhaps the galling pity bestowed on her by her fellow residents was another reason for Clara Mortimer's reserve, Rafferty reasoned, before Amelia Frobisher spoke again.

With an air of reluctance, she told them, 'Though, having said that we all look out for one another, I have to add that, as warden, Mrs Atkins isn't always as careful as she might be.'

Here we go again, Rafferty thought as he waited to learn what other piece of 'family' tittle-tattle he was about to hear, though in a murder inquiry, he was more than happy to listen as the combatants poured out their grievances. In spite of the grievances, he thought it likely they *did* look out for one another as she claimed. Though if the 'Mat Wars' and the 'Freddy Talbot Spat' were indicative, they also appeared to share a real family's inclinations towards bickering, spite and grudge-holding.

He guessed from her expression that Amelia Frobisher was about to indulge in the second of these woeful family tendencies and claim payback – from Rita Atkins at least.

'Of course, you know, Inspector, poor Mrs Atkins has a little problem.'

As though she suspected eavesdroppers concealed behind her flounced arras, Miss Frobisher confided in a conspiratorial stage whisper, 'She *drinks*. It's what makes her turn from quiet and meek into loud and vulgar. I understand she feels offended that I have never included her in our little theatrical soirées with the rest of the residents of the block. But I mean – how could one? Since you chose to speak to her first, before coming to see me' – another grievance? Rafferty wondered – 'you must have noticed the smell of whisky on her breath, even this early in the day. Who is to know what kind of an exhibition she would make of herself – and us – if she decided to make free of the bar during one of our theatre trips?'

Amelia Frobisher shook her head as though to indicate she spoke more in sorrow than condemnation, though whether this was a true reflection of her feelings Rafferty was inclined to doubt. Like Rita Atkins, Miss Frobisher was another who chose indiscretion.

A degree of sensitivity might have reflected better on both of them, Rafferty thought. Though as a policeman with a murder to solve, he was just grateful that, thus far, the residents he had interviewed had seemed to feel his ears suitable receptacles for their outpourings.

And this latest outpouring provided one possible solution as to how the intruder had gained admission. If Rita

Atkins was as careless as Miss Frobisher had implied, she might have left the front door unsecured. Though that still didn't explain how the murderer had gained access to Clara Mortimer's apartment.

Amelia Frobisher's next words went some way to explaining what might have happened.

'Of course, as warden, Mrs Atkins keeps skeleton keys to each of the apartments as a security measure in case any resident living alone should press the panic button and she needed to let the emergency services in.'

Rita Atkins had not only failed to mention if any of the sets of skeleton keys had gone missing – she hadn't mentioned them at all.

At a nod from Rafferty, Llewellyn slipped from the room to obtain an answer to this question. He was back in less than five minutes. His shake of the head to Rafferty indicated all the skeleton keys were present and correct.

'I presume the panic bells sound in the warden's apartment?' Rafferty now asked.

Miss Frobisher nodded. 'I have to say, that in spite of the drinking, Mrs Atkins always answers the bell. I can't fault her on that.'

From the wistful note in her voice, Rafferty guessed she would have liked to. He wondered how the other residents felt about her 'adoption' of them. From what she had said about Clara Mortimer's refusal to join them on their excursions, it sounded as if Mrs Mortimer, at least, hadn't much relished being gathered to Amelia Frobisher's flat bosom.

'I know Mrs Atkins claimed that Clara didn't press the panic button,' Miss Frobisher mused aloud. 'There are several in each room. You're always within a few paces of one or the other.' She eyed them speculatively before she suggested, 'But there's a first time for everything, and I did rather wonder, if on this occasion, and given our warden's unfortunate and increasing habit, whether she simply didn't hear the bell and slept through it . . .'

Amelia Frobisher didn't pursue the subject further. She had planted the seed. Now she could wait to let the idea take root that it was owing to Rita's drunken stupor that Clara Mortimer had died and died all alone.

In fact, Clara Mortimer's body had been right beside one of these panic buttons. Had she frozen in fright, as he had earlier thought likely? Or had her attacker knocked her unconscious before she had had time to react?

As they took their leave of Amelia Frobisher and returned to Clara Mortimer's apartment, he put the question to Llewellyn.

As usual, his sergeant had a logical explanation.

'Perhaps Mrs Mortimer was unwilling to risk Rita Atkins being attacked when she came to check on her? Given her small stature, it's not as if Mrs Atkins would be much assistance against a determined assailant.'

'Maybe so. But a stranger couldn't know for sure *who* would respond to the panic alarm,' Rafferty pointed out. 'If she *had* pressed it, he would have been more likely to flee to stop himself being apprehended than to wait and see if a Mr Burly turned up. Nobody's suggested Clara Mortimer was stupid, so she must have realized that pressing the alarm was her best chance to save herself.'

Llewellyn shrugged and repeated Rafferty's earlier thought. 'She probably just froze. People do.'

Rafferty said no more. But the picture of Clara Mortimer that was already building in his mind didn't suggest she had been the type of woman to freeze in fright. On the contrary, she hadn't been scared to tackle her daughter's boyfriend and accuse him of stealing from her or to tell the importunate Freddie Talbot to take a hike.

The determinedly solitary Clara Mortimer, with her estrangement from her real family and her rejection of the one that had attempted to adopt her, was beginning to intrigue him.

Three

Rafferty set Llewellyn the task of organizing a house-to-house of the neighbouring streets as well as making a start on the preliminary interviews of the other residents. In the hope that at least one possible suspect would be eliminated early in the proceedings, he sent DC Hanks off to speak to Freddie Talbot and get his statement as to his whereabouts this morning.

While Llewellyn got on with the routine tasks, Rafferty used his mobile to contact the station and arrange for DS Mary Carmody to meet him in Mercer's Lane to break the news of Clara Mortimer's murder to her daughter, Jane Ogilvie.

Mary Carmody, although only in her thirties, had a comforting, motherly air about her. She would, Rafferty knew, as he left the scene and turned right into the High Street to walk the two hundred yards to Mercer's Lane, be a staunch support in the hours that followed.

DS Mary Carmody was waiting in her car a few houses up from No 12 when Rafferty arrived. Carmody got out of her car and approached him.

'I checked the daughter's name and street number,' she told him. 'According to the neighbours, she's still calling herself Mrs Ogilvie. The current live-in boyfriend's called Darryl Jesmond. They're squatting at number twelve, I gather.' She nodded at a rusty blue Rover that was parked haphazardly about eighteen inches from the kerb. 'The neighbour told me that vehicle belongs to Jane Ogilvie, so it's likely she's at home.'

Rafferty nodded. The careless parking in the narrow street of mean Victorian terraces added to the sum total he had gathered of Jane Ogilvie's character. So far all of it was negative. But as he wouldn't like his own character to be assassinated by the likes of Rita Atkins and Amelia Frobisher without benefit of self-defence, he put aside their sweeping judgements and prepared to keep an open mind and listen to what Jane Ogilvie had to say.

Together, he and Mary Carmody approached the house. Like Jane Ogilvie's car, the house had seen better days. No wonder she and her boyfriend had tried currying favour with Mrs Mortimer. Plumb in the middle of the terraced row, their squat looked originally to have been a family house, but the two floors had been broken up into flats. Although No 12A's front door had received a recent coat of paint, that of No 12 looked as if, snakelike, it was in the process of shedding a skin, as, in parts, a thin coating of orange paint still adhered, whereas in others, the bare wood was clearly visible. Unlike its neighbour, the door had neither knocker nor letterbox, just a gaping hole where someone had roughly wrenched them off, splintering the wood in the process.

Rafferty was beginning to wonder if Jane Ogilvie had been an *adopted* daughter. It was possible. Certainly none of the late Clara Mortimer's fellow residents had been able to give them any more than the most cursory information about her; a fact that had clearly rankled with one or two of them.

He knocked on the door and waited, curious to see the elegant, late Clara Mortimer's slovenly daughter in the flesh.

But it seemed the scratching of that particular itch would have to wait because the door was opened by a youngish man whom Rafferty presumed must be the toy-boy boyfriend, Darryl Jesmond.

Jesmond looked around twenty-eight. Unless Clara

Mortimer had given birth to her daughter very late, Jesmond, as Rita Atkins and Amelia Frobisher had said, must surely be some years Jane Ogilvie's junior. A good-looking young man, who appeared aware of it, Jesmond carried himself with a cocky, challenging air, his arms carried flexed and away from his body.

Although the June day was chilly, Jesmond wore a white, sleeveless T-shirt with the pair of tight blue jeans that had made Amelia Frobisher's eyes pop. The T-shirt showed off the muscular torso, as no doubt was intended. And although the state of the outside of the flat indicated a paucity of ready cash, Jesmond's skin glowed from a recent bask under a southern sun – unless the tan came from a bottle? He certainly appeared vain enough to use fake tan.

Jesmond looked Rafferty and Mary Carmody up and down. Then, having taken in the suits, he made a wrong assumption and immediately told them, 'The instalment for the fine's in the post. I posted it myself, so if you—'

'We're not here about a fine, Mr Jesmond,' Rafferty told him. Intrigued, he made a mental note to check what the fine had been for.

Some play of shadow across Jesmond's features made Rafferty feel he was well aware of who they were. Perhaps he had good reason to recognize police officers when he saw them. Rafferty wondered if Jesmond had a criminal record of the more serious kind. It was something else to get checked out at the earliest opportunity.

Certainly, it seemed unlikely that Jesmond supported himself with legally earned income, given that he was at home in the middle of the morning and didn't wear the jaded air or pale skin of a night-worker.

'We're police officers.' Rafferty confirmed what he thought Jesmond already suspected, before introducing himself and DS Carmody. 'We'd like to speak to Mrs Jane Ogilvie, who we believe lives here. It's about her mother, Mrs Clara Mortimer.'

'What's that old bitch been saying about me now?' Jesmond demanded belligerently. 'If she's accusing me of stealing from her again, I'll—'

Again, Rafferty wondered whether this show of belligerence was used to conceal some other emotion. If Jesmond had had anything to do with Mrs Mortimer's death, he could have decided that such a show of aggression towards the victim would be a clever after-the-act move to put on for the investigating officers.

'Mrs Mortimer's not in a position to accuse anyone of anything, Mr Jesmond,' Rafferty told him flatly. 'That's why we're here. We've some bad news for Mrs Ogilvie concerning her mother.'

Darryl Jesmond suddenly became much less voluble. He gazed suspiciously at them from narrowed eyes before he told them, 'Jane's not here. She's at work.'

'When do you expect her back? Only, we do need to see her as a matter of urgency.'

'Why?' He frowned. 'You said it was about the old woman. Urgent. That can only mean one thing. She's dead, isn't she? The old girl, I mean?'

He gazed at them triumphantly, as if expecting them to congratulate him on his perspicacity.

Again, Rafferty wondered if this parade of questions and self-provided answers were gone through merely for their benefit. But perhaps he was being unduly cynical.

Rafferty neither confirmed nor denied Clara Mortimer's death, but simply repeated his question as to when Jane Ogilvie was expected home.

Jesmond shrugged. 'Your guess is as good as mine. She should have been back ages ago. She got herself a night job a few months back, stacking shelves at the supermarket. I suppose you'd better come in and wait,' he invited ungraciously as he turned away and headed back up the narrow hallway.

Rafferty and Mary Carmody followed Jesmond down a

hallway that was partly bare brick where plaster had fallen from the walls. It was littered with bags of overflowing rubbish that were beginning to smell; clearly the household had failed to rise early enough to put their rubbish out on the allocated collection day.

'Surely you have a phone number for her?' Rafferty asked as he just avoided the last, precariously placed and bursting bag of rubbish and entered the back living room.

'Of course I've got a phone number for her. It's just that our phone's out of order.'

Been cut off, more like, thought Rafferty as he pulled out his mobile. 'If you can give me the number?'

After Jesmond had rummaged for a minute in a cupboard drawer crowded with flyers from local take-away restaurants and cards for mini-cab firms, he finally located the scrap of paper. But before he could give it to Rafferty, a key turned in the front door and a harassed-looking woman he assumed must be Jane Ogilvie opened the door and saved him the trouble.

As skinny as a teenager and with long, straggly, badly bleached hair that only served to emphasize the lack of a youthful bloom to her skin, she appeared to be trying – and failing – to hold back the years. No wonder, with the much younger Jesmond for a live-in partner, that she should look harassed; Rafferty could imagine Darryl Jesmond would make the women in his life jump through hoops for his benefit. A night spent stacking supermarket shelves was even less likely to increase a woman's bloom, certainly not one who looked, like Rafferty himself, to be on the fast track to forty and whose bloom had now to be applied from a tube.

Jane Ogilvie was trailed by a young man in his early twenties who wore a smart and expensive-looking light-grey executive's suit, with a jaded, over-stressed, executive's demeanour. He was carrying a suitcase that wasn't a match for the smart suit. But even with the shabby case, he looked as out of place in the scruffy family home as a sleek, just-off-the-assembly-line limousine in a used-car lot.

Rafferty, wondering if this latest arrival was another one, albeit more up-market, of Jane's toy boys, thought his guess confirmed when Jesmond, with a glower, took in the other young man's suitcase.

'What the hell—?' he began.

'Please don't have a go, Darryl,' Jane said hurriedly, her tone placatory. 'This is my son, Charles. I said he can stay for a few days.'

Darryl stared at her as if he thought she was losing her wits. 'I know who he is, for Christ's sake. How could I not?' he demanded.

This last was a surprisingly reasonable question from Jesmond, who had the looks of a man who took unreasonableness to an art form. For, as Rafferty himself had already noted, the living room revealed that in matters of family sentiment, Jane chose the opposite course to her mother.

Pictures of her children held a prominent, no *defiant* place, as if she was determined to ram the fact of their existence down her mother's throat even though Jane must have known how unlikely it was that the far more fastidious Clara Mortimer would ever set foot over the threshold of the squat.

As he gazed from toddler photographs through to those of sulky teens, he managed to work out that Jane had three children. They comprised one white son, one mixed-race daughter and another son of Middle Eastern cast. Clearly, Amelia Frobisher hadn't known how widely Jane Ogilvie had spread her favours; if she had, her comments would've been likely to make even the defiant Jane's ears burn.

Rafferty was surprised to discover that the smart-as-paint young man was Jane's son; as he had already observed, the smart-suited Charles didn't look as if he belonged in his mother's run-down and borrowed home. He had changed quite a bit from the boy in his last, teenaged photo. The chubbiness of adolescence had vanished as had the mud and the football strip and, though the teenage tendency to pimples remained, pallor had replaced the healthy colour of the sporty schoolboy.

'As I said,' Darryl's belligerent voice butted into Rafferty's musings. 'I know *who* he is. What I want to know is why—?'

Jane cut him off. 'Please don't make a scene, Dazza,' she pleaded. 'You know I haven't seen him for months.' Her voice, full of earnest entreaty, continued to coax. 'He'll only be here for a few days. I know we weren't expecting him, but it was a spur of the moment visit before he starts his new job. He'll be no trouble.'

Darryl opened his mouth as if about to say 'he'd better not be'. But instead, after a glance at Rafferty, he shrugged and shut his mouth as if he had just remembered that Jane had more pressing problems to face than placating him over their unexpected house guest.

He jerked his head towards Rafferty and Mary Carmody. 'You've got visitors. Coppers. They want to speak to you about your old mother,' he told her bluntly.

Jane blinked and turned from Darryl to stare warily at them.

The wayward Jane's wary expression caused Rafferty to wonder whether Darryl Jesmond might not be the only one to have crossed swords with the courts and the criminal justice system.

'What do you want?' Jane asked Rafferty as she pulled off the uncomfortable-looking high heels that were so unsuitable for a shelf-stacking job and slumped wearily on the stained green settee. She pushed her hands through already disordered hair and told him with teenage petulance, 'I've just finished a long night shift and I'm bushed. Can't it wait, whatever it is?'

Rafferty hesitated. He was conscious that concerning Jane's relationship with her murdered mother, he had only heard half the story and that half might be unfairly prejudiced against a

Jane, who, to Clara Mortimer's apartment block contemporaries, must seem challengingly unconventional.

'I'm sorry,' he said. 'But no, it can't wait. I'm afraid we have bad news regarding your mother, Mrs Clara Mortimer.'

Jane's gaze flickered from Rafferty to Mary Carmody, to Darryl, then to her son, before it settled back on Rafferty. 'What about my mother?'

'As I said, Mrs Ogilvie, it's bad news. You should prepare yourself for a shock.'

Rafferty tentatively sat opposite her on the edge of a green armchair that was a stained match for the settee. He waited as her son dropped the suitcase in the corner and sat next to his mother on the arm of the settee as if hoping to shield her from the bad news that was obviously coming.

'Your mother was found dead earlier this morning in her apartment on Priory Way,' Rafferty told her gently. 'It looks like she disturbed an intruder.'

Jane's lips formed the words *an intruder*, as if she couldn't quite grasp his meaning. Once again, her gaze went from face to face as if seeking further enlightenment.

Rafferty explained. 'I'm sorry to have to tell you this, but your mother suffered a fatal head injury. One of her neighbours found her.'

Jane took a few moments to absorb this. Then she said simply, 'I see.' She fixed Rafferty with an abstracted eye. 'This neighbour,' she began. 'Did they see anything? Were they able to tell you who might have attacked my mother?'

'I'm afraid not. We believe your mother had already been dead for around an hour when the neighbour noticed her apartment door was ajar. She investigated and found your mother.'

Jane drew in a deep, shuddering breath and slumped back in her chair.

'I'm sorry to have to ask further questions at such a difficult time, but is there anyone else we need to contact? Your mother lived alone. Her husband?'

Jane took a few seconds to drag herself back from shock. 'He's dead,' she told him briefly. 'My father died some years ago.'

Glad to get confirmation of this, Rafferty sat back. He noticed Darryl Jesmond open his mouth again, but he obviously thought better of whatever he had been going to say, because again he shut it without saying anything. Clearly, he wasn't a young man gifted with the ability to comfort the bereaved. Neither, for that matter, was Jane's son. But, at least Charles Ogilvie, his face a greenish grey, put a trembling hand on his mother's shoulder in an awkward attempt to offer comfort. His touch was tentative, as if he feared the mercurial-seeming Jane would reject it and the comfort he was trying to provide.

Charles Ogilvie seemed far more affected by the news of his grandmother's violent death than did his mother, Rafferty observed. This young man struck him as being more in need of comfort than the still dry-eyed Jane. From his fine-hewn features and nervy air, Rafferty judged him a sensitive lad. But he was young yet and, unlike Jane who had already lost her father, the violent death of his grandmother was likely to be his first contact with mortality.

Suddenly, Charles's face looked even more stricken and he asked, 'What about my brother and sister? Who's going to break the news to them?' His sensitive face turned even greyer as he voiced the question.

Rafferty asked where they were.

Jane answered. 'They're at school. If they're there, that is, and not bunking off.'

Charles clarified his mother's answer. 'They go to St Vincent's. My sister's name is Aurora Mortimer and my brother's name is Hakim Mohammed Abdullah. His father's Arab,' he unnecessarily explained what Rafferty had already surmised from the many photographs.

Rita Atkins's talk of Jane's children being something of a Heinz 57 varieties wasn't far out, thought Rafferty. He wondered what the children thought about all having different fathers.

But as the thoughts of Jane's other children on such a matter seemed unlikely to be confided to a policeman, far less one they had yet to meet, Rafferty put aside such pointless musings, took out his mobile, rang the station and arranged for the children to be collected in an hour's time and brought back home.

After what he had so far learned of Clara Mortimer's relationship with her daughter Rafferty wasn't surprised that Jane had remained dry-eyed at the news of her mother's murder.

But now, as if she had only just taken it in – or was doing what she must consider expected in the circumstances – she surprised him by bursting into tears and flinging herself into her son's arms. Charles looked horrified.

Rafferty thought for a moment or two that he was going to thrust his weeping mother away from him, as if all this sudden emotional drama was more than he could cope with. But after that brief drawing back, he hugged Jane as tightly as any mother could wish. It was some time before Jane calmed down sufficiently in order to be told the rest.

Rafferty noted that, in spite of her storm of weeping, there were few marks of tears on her cheeks. But before he could take this thought to a natural destination, Rafferty remembered he had sworn to give up jumping to conclusions before he had any facts to back them up. Besides, it was possible that she thought he was unaware of the family estrangement and felt obliged to supply the tears such a sudden bereavement warranted.

While Jane Ogilvie indulged in unnecessary mopping-up operations, Rafferty tipped the wink to Mary Carmody to check whether the mortuary was ready for them.

A few minutes later, DS Carmody slipped back in to the room and gave him the nod.

Rafferty turned to Jane. 'Do you feel up to identifying your mother now, Mrs Ogilvie?'

'Me?' Clearly appalled at such a responsibility, Jane appealed to her eldest son. 'You do it, Charlie. You were her favourite grandchild. At least you used to be.'

Charles Ogilvie blanched. His skin went the colour of tallow. And at his mother's repeated urging that he take on the unwelcome duty, he blurted out, 'But you're forgetting, Mum, I haven't seen her since I was a kid. How can I identify her?'

Jane frowned at this. She pursed her lips as the realization dawned on her that there was no escaping the duty of identifying her mother.

'Silly of me. I forgot.'

Rafferty intervened. 'It does need to be someone who is familiar with the deceased.' He addressed his next remark to Jane. 'I understand you last saw her around a week ago?'

Jane flushed, tossed her stringy blonde mane and unwisely blurted out the first thing that came in to her head. 'I suppose you've heard all about the falling-out Darryl had with my mother?'

'There was something of the sort mentioned,' Rafferty murmured as he took in the look of venom Jane's unthinking remark extracted from her toy boy. There were more undercurrents here than in the River Thames, he thought.

Angry colour enlivened Jane's previous washed-out pallor. 'Those old women – got nothing better to do than poke their noses into my business; judging me, always judging me, just like—'

Her angry voice broke off abruptly, though the heightened colour in her previously pale cheeks remained as a reminder that Jane had a ready temper.

Her boyfriend also didn't look the type to turn the other cheek. The half smirk that seemed to be his normal expression had, at Jane's revelation about the row, been replaced by a ferocious scowl.

As if unaware that, in confirming the aggressive Darryl had had a recent falling out with her murdered mother she had placed him squarely at the top of their suspect list, Jane sat, staring blindly into space.

But perhaps her staring wasn't so blind. Perhaps now she was seeing that her bitterness against her mother was up against the final, slamming door of death, because Jane's next words revealed remorse that the estrangement between herself and her mother should reflect badly on Clara Mortimer.

'Whenever I visited Mum I would feel eyes watching me, scrutinizing me from behind their oh-so-clean nets, damning me for not being more like they expected Clara's daughter to be. I always thought they kept such a lookout so they could know who had visitors and who didn't and do a bit of crowing. Spiteful old bitches. Just so they could get one over on each other.'

From where he was leaning, oh-so-casually against the doorpost, Darryl Jesmond put aside his scowl, ran his hand through his blond-streaked, floppy, light-brown hair and remarked with a faint smile that held more than a hint of self-satisfaction, 'Yeah, I felt that, too – eyes watching me every time I visited. It gave me the creeps to think of all those old wrinklies using me to enliven their dreams.'

Rafferty suspected that, secretly, Darryl had got a kick out of it. If the ladies of the sheltered apartments *had* watched him, as he claimed, it would only confirm for Darryl how justified was his self-love. He certainly hadn't expressed any concern for Jane in her bereavement.

This thought seemed to strike Jane at the same time it struck Rafferty, for she rounded on Darryl.

'You!' she said scornfully. 'It's always about you, isn't it? *I'm* the one who's just lost her mother,' she reminded him.

'Yeah,' he drawled carelessly. 'Like it's as if you gave a toss for the old bag.'

Jane, about to make another retort, clenched her lips tight shut on whatever she had been going to say, as if realizing with what fascination the police audience were following the exchange.

Rafferty, regretfully accepting that they were to hear no more intriguing revelations, took the opportunity the sudden silence afforded to answer Jane's earlier complaint.

'Just to reassure you, I don't listen to tittle-tattle,' Rafferty told her.

'No?' Clearly she didn't believe him. 'You must be the only person in the world who doesn't then.' She put her still-dry tissue in her pocket and stood up. 'Hadn't we better get along to the mortuary? I'll need to break the news to my other children also, so the sooner I identify her, the sooner I can do so.' She took her son's hand in a grip so fierce that Charlie visibly winced. 'I'll do the identifying, but I want you to accompany me.'

For a moment or two, it looked as though Charles would refuse his mother's demand.

Rafferty would have excused him on the grounds of youth alone and was surprised Jane didn't insist Darryl Jesmond accompanied her. Unless you were PC Smales, whose uniform demanded his attendance, a mortuary was no place for the young.

Rafferty was about to say something along these lines when Charles visibly swallowed past the lump in his throat and gave his reluctant agreement.

Once Jane had identified Clara Mortimer's body and she and her son had returned to the car for the journey home, they both became very quiet. In spite of his grown-up executive suit Charles looked even younger than the twenty odd years Rafferty gave him by the time their painful duty was concluded.

It was only as Rafferty pulled up outside her front door that Jane Ogilvie released the flood of emotions that must have been simmering inside since learning of her mother's death – or possibly, Rafferty guessed as he listened to the stored resentments pour out, for years before that.

'*Jane* – why did she have to call me that? Jane. Plain Jane. I've always resented her for it and for the fact that she'd never thought I might *be* plain. I was teased with that *Plain Jane* tag all through my schooldays and beyond. But Mum – *Mother*, as she always insisted I call her, never understood that not everyone had her stiff-upper-lip stoicism.'

She directed a defiant stare at Rafferty, who had half-turned round in the front passenger seat and challenged him. 'I suppose you think I'm an awful daughter? You must do if you've been listening to the spite those old women at the apartments must have poured in your ears all morning.'

'I've generally found there are two sides to every story,' he told her quietly.

'Yeah, right. And you don't listen to gossip, either, do you?' She gave an unladylike snort and for a few moments she seemed to retreat into private memories which, moments later, she decided to share with the motherly Mary Carmody, whose warm maternal features so often invited unwise confidences.

'I suppose I started becoming rebellious when I was about thirteen. I'm not sure even now if I got pregnant that first time with Charles when I was in my late teens just to spite my mother. I spited her all right. She didn't talk to me for six weeks. She was like that, my mother. She'd give you the silent treatment. Unfortunately for her, she didn't realize I preferred the silent treatment to the reproachful criticisms which I got when I was merely exasperating her. Anyway, my boyfriend, Charlie's dad, married me and I became Mrs Ogilvie. I was respectable then.

'The marriage didn't last, of course; perhaps I didn't want it to as such conformity was way too pleasing to my mother.'

Beside her, in the back seat of the car, as if worried she might be incriminating herself, her son tried to quieten her.

'Mum, you shouldn't talk like that. Not after —' Charles took one glance at Rafferty and broke off.

Not after her mother had died such a violent death, Rafferty imagined Charles Ogilvie had been going to say. It was good advice, too. But it had no discernible effect on his mother, who continued her unwise outpourings.

'After me and my husband split I took up with different men. I had a fling with an Arab man and got pregnant again with my little Hakim Mohammed. By the time I'd had the third kid, my daughter, Aurora, with the local bad lad black drug dealer, the silent treatment was beyond her. She refused even to see me after that, never mind *speak* to me.'

Jane gave a humourless laugh. 'I was an embarrassment, you see, a social embarrassment. I'd pissed on her image of herself, brought her down. She can't . . . couldn't, forgive that.' Her voice had become little more than a whisper as she added, 'And now . . . now, she never will.'

It seemed her son's words of warning had at last penetrated, for Jane stared at them from eyes that dared them to criticize her. Their very challenge revealed more of her vulnerability than copious tears ever could.

'Apart from having and bringing up my kids, that's the only thing I've ever achieved in life – hurting her. In two generations, I've managed to drag her family line down from the manor house and its gentle living, where she started life, to this squalid squat –' she nodded towards the peeling, vandalized front door of her 'borrowed' flat – 'and two half-caste grandchildren.'

For a moment, her face slackened as if in realization that such an achievement wasn't up there with climbing Everest. Then, as if shrugging off this acknowledgement, she bared stained smoker's teeth in a Grim Reaper's smile, and said, 'The squat could be erased from the family history, but the half-caste family line can't. She might have denied two of her grandchildren in life, but in death she can't deny them. Her descendants won't let her. My two youngest kids' surnames are their own testimony.' It was clear she believed it to be a triumph of sorts.

Rafferty felt like asking her if she didn't think it was time that she grew up and took responsibility for her own actions. But he said nothing, not least because he was honest enough to admit to himself that, in wrestling with his own concerns about responsibility, he wasn't exactly rushing to embrace the mature grown-up world himself.

When Jane's complaints finally ran down, she stared at her closed front door, then, with an air of reluctance, she climbed from the car. And as she opened the door and it was rushed by two youngsters – a pretty young mixed-race girl around twelve or thirteen and a handsome youth in his mid-teens, whose proud features proclaimed his Middle Eastern paternity – Rafferty offered Jane the silent commiseration he had been unable to voice before. After a full night shift, Jane Ogilvie must have been exhausted; yet now she faced the task of breaking the grim news to her two younger children.

Hit by an attack of conscience after his earlier feelings of dislike, Rafferty got out of the car and offered to leave Mary Carmody with her in order to provide the support it was clear Darryl Jesmond wouldn't supply. But his offer was curtly declined and as the WPC who had collected the two younger children from school came to the door, she was unceremoniously bustled out and the door was all but slammed in their faces.

'Well honestly,' remarked young WPC Allen. 'The manners of some people.'

'She *has* just had a shock,' Mary Carmody gently reminded the younger officer. She glanced at Rafferty. 'But, even so, I don't think she or the boyfriend merit removal from the suspect list just yet, do you, sir?'

Rafferty shrugged and gave his best imitation of the cautious Llewellyn. 'It's early days. It wouldn't do to jump to any hasty conclusions.'

This comment brought a stunned silence, not only from Mary Carmody – who knew of his famous predilection for leaping ahead of the game and the evidence, but also from WPC Allen, who was a recent addition to the Force, but who had obviously made it her business to tune into canteen gossip.

Rafferty, with his newly adopted caution about such matters, felt put out that no one had even noticed it. To hide this, he remarked acerbically, 'Well, if the recently bereaved Mrs Ogilvie doesn't require our services, I'm sure we're all got plenty to be getting on with.'

Acknowledging the dismissal, WPC Allen shot a rueful glance at Mary Carmody and made for her car.

After a moment's hesitation, Mary Carmody did likewise, leaving Rafferty to bring up the rear. And as he climbed in the passenger seat, having concluded that his walk to Mercer's Lane had given him enough exercise for one day, he couldn't help but reflect that after being in Jane Ogilvie's company for the best part of an hour, it would be a relief to get back to the murder scene.

As Carmody pulled away from the kerb, Rafferty gazed thoughtfully out the window. It was clear that Clara Mortimer's daughter had an enormous chip on her shoulder. Was it justified? he wondered. Or was she truly the grown woman who refused to grow up that she appeared to be? Couldn't she see that the person most damaged by her rebellious behaviour had been herself?

But, as Rafferty turned and stared back at the peeling front door of Jane Ogilvie's flat, he was filled with a profound sadness for Clara Mortimer that her immediate family had shed barely a tear at her passing.

Four

On arrival back at the police station, Rafferty hurried to his office. He was anxious to read the preliminary reports from the house-to-house teams.

But as he discovered, these early reports added up to very little, which wasn't altogether surprising as Sam Dally had said Clara Mortimer had died around 7.00 a.m.: a time when most people would either have been still in bed or just getting up and preparing themselves for another day.

Disappointed, he headed back to the scene, hoping Llewellyn's interviews of the other residents might have unearthed something more interesting.

He found Llewellyn outside the Priory Way apartment block organizing yet another team. When he saw Rafferty, he dismissed the officers, made a brief note on the sheaf of papers he held on the clipboard he kept handy in his car, and walked towards him.

As Llewellyn explained what had so far been accomplished, Rafferty nodded his approval. Llewellyn had done well in his absence. Not only had the teams he'd organized nearly finished the house-to-house in the streets in the immediate vicinity, they had also discovered the identities of the early-morning dog-walkers in the park opposite the block and had already spoken to several of these as well as the apartments' gardeners and interviewed almost all of the rest of the residents of the sheltered apartments.

'Anything of any consequence come out yet?' Rafferty

asked hopefully as he sat on the low York-stone wall that encircled the block and gazed across to the park.

Llewellyn sat beside him. 'We've made one or two interesting discoveries from the other residents. The only residents we haven't yet been able to interview are a Mr Hal Oliver, who only moved into a small, third-floor apartment a couple of weeks ago, and a Mr Toombes. Mr Oliver's away from home at present, but I understand he's expected back later today.

'As for Mr Toombes, according to his wife, he went out fishing first thing this morning and has not yet returned.

'By the way, I've had confirmation from another resident that Mrs Mortimer's daughter's boyfriend, Darryl Jesmond, had a row with the victim around a week ago.'

'Touché,' said Rafferty. 'I've had confirmation from a third source; no less than the victim's daughter herself. Darryl Jesmond didn't look very happy about it. For a moment there I thought there might be another murder done.'

Llewellyn looked thoughtful for a second, then he asked, 'Did he strike you as a man who would be foolish enough, only one week later, to kill a person with whom he had a very public argument?'

'Mr Jesmond struck me as cocky and overconfident, so it's possible. There again, as he's managed to acquire a nice tan with no job and presumably, given the way he and Jane Ogilvie live, no private income either, he must have more than his share of street wisdom. Ring Bill Beard and get him to run Jarrold and Jane Ogilvie through the computer. For that matter, get him to run them all through the computer, including Freddie Talbot and, when we find out their names, the fathers of Mrs Ogilvie's two younger children whose identities I forgot to establish.'

Once Llewellyn had come off the phone after giving Beard his instructions, Rafferty said, 'Now, tell me about these interesting discoveries you mentioned.'

Llewellyn told him that one of the residents, a Mrs Toombes, had said that somebody had rung her and her husband's apartment bell that morning at around 6.45. Mrs Toombes, who had answered the ring, had thought little of it at the time and it was only later, on being interviewed, that she had mentioned it to Llewellyn.

Mr and Mrs Toombes lived in one of the five smaller apartments on the third floor, the one immediately above that of the victim. Mrs Toombes, to judge from the nervous chatter with which she greeted them after they had taken the three flights of stairs to the top floor and knocked on her door, was no longer in any doubt about the possible significance of her information. She seemed to have worked herself into something of a nervous state about it.

Mrs Toombes was a large, ungainly woman and her anxiety struck a jarring note as if it sat uncomfortably in her slow-moving body.

After several minutes of earnest lamentations about the late Clara Mortimer and the repeated wish that her husband would return home, she urged them into her main room, a small lounge-diner, cluttered with the usual three-piece suite with a small, folding oak table in the window. A 28" television dominated the room and not only by virtue of its size for it was currently loudly blaring out some daytime quiz show.

Mrs Toombes turned the set off and invited them to sit down. Then, clearly troubled, she confirmed what Llewellyn had already told him.

'I've been wondering since if it was the killer trying to gain entrance here,' she confided. In her agitation, her large hands clutched at one another. 'Imagine, if I'd opened the door, it might have been *me* he killed, rather than poor Clara Mortimer.'

'What did he say, this man when you answered the entry-phone?' Rafferty asked Mrs Toombes. 'Can you remember?'

Obviously still upset and fixated on the fact that Clara's

fate could so easily have been *hers*, Mrs Toombes frowned and asked him to repeat his question.

When he did so, she bridled. 'Of course I can remember.' His question seemed to annoy her. Her voice was raised as she replied. 'There's nothing wrong with my memory. I haven't been able to get his words out of my head. They sounded so ordinary, so normal. That's what's so strange.'

'I can appreciate how upset you must feel, Mrs Toombes. But if you could just let us know what he actually said?'

'I'm coming to that. Please don't try to rush me. My husband's always doing it and it always gets me flustered.' She paused, stared at the silent TV with a frown as if she missed its loud companionship. Having gathered her thoughts, she went on. 'Anyway, he seemed to be looking for someone called Esme. He must have been late because he seemed keen for this Esme to know that he had hurried. "I ran, Esme," he said.

'I told him that he not only had the wrong apartment, but the wrong block, because I know there is no woman named Esme living here.

'He didn't even thank me for putting him right,' she complained. 'He just put the phone down on me. I thought no more about it till I learned that Mrs Mortimer had been murdered.' She shivered at the realization that she, rather than Clara Mortimer, might have been the murderer's chosen victim.

'Did you get any idea as to this man's age?' Rafferty asked.

'Not really, no. Though it wasn't the voice of an elderly man. Other than that, he could have been any age up to his forties.'

Defensively, as if she felt he was criticizing her, she added, 'He *did* only say three words.'

Rafferty forced a smile. 'Never mind. Maybe something else will strike you about this man in due course.'

Mrs Toombes's 'Maybe' sounded even less confident than Rafferty's.

After Rafferty and Llewellyn had thanked Mrs Toombes and departed, they had a quiet conference on the landing.

'What do you think, Dafyd? That some tearaway was ringing bells at random to see if anyone was foolish enough to let him in?'

'They may well have been,' Llewellyn observed. 'But it seems doubtful that Mrs Mortimer would have been so foolish as to do so. From what we've learned of her, she didn't seem to be the type of trusting old lady who becomes a victim of crime.'

'No. That's what I thought, too. But she's become a victim of crime all the same, so I don't think we can totally discount the possibility.'

Rafferty's lips pursed. 'Wonder why this early-morning bell-ringer should have hit on the name *Esme* as the preferred open-sesame. It's hardly a common name, even amongst elderly ladies.'

'Certainly, none of the female residents of this block bear such a name, not even as a middle name.' Llewellyn confirmed Mrs Toombes's claim. 'And none of the other residents reported anyone ringing their apartment bells early this morning. I've wondered if this man didn't just start at the top bell on the left, which is the one to the Toombes's apartment and then moved down to Mrs Mortimer's, which is the next in line.'

'And struck pay-dirt, you mean?'

Llewellyn nodded. 'Of course, the difficulty with that is the character of Mrs Mortimer.'

'Mm. That is a bit of a poser,' Rafferty agreed. 'For a woman who refused to socialize with her neighbours to be willing to so naively open her door in the early morning, strikes against all reason. On the other hand, she *is* dead and dead because of a violent assault.'

He sighed and made for the stairs, followed by Llewellyn. 'Perhaps we're expecting complications when the case is not complicated at all. Maybe it *is* as simple as a lonely woman letting her guard down and paying the ultimate price.'

Rafferty paused, then asked, 'Apart from Mr Oliver and Mr Toombes, have all the residents been questioned?'

'Yes.' Llewellyn broke off as they reached the ground-floor lobby and DC Jonathon Lilley approached for a quick word with him. 'But I gather Mr Oliver's returned home now. I instructed Lilley here to get a statement from him on his return. But perhaps you'd prefer to speak to him yourself?'

Rafferty glanced at his watch. He was surprised to find it was almost 6.00 p.m. Tempted to make an early finish, Rafferty remembered he was meant to have altered his laissez-faire attitudes. If he abandoned such an alteration so soon after the change, no one would *ever* notice it.

'Why not?' he asked. 'Though, seeing as Mr Oliver was away from home at the relevant time, it's unlikely he'll be able to tell us anything. Still, it's always best to be thorough and in view of the red roses Mrs Atkins claimed he presented to the victim, now seems like a good time to ask him about his relationship with Mrs Mortimer.'

Llewellyn nodded and made for the stairs once more. Just in time, Rafferty remembered that, like the Toombses, Hal Oliver lived on the third floor. No way was he traipsing up all those stairs again. He called to Llewellyn, 'Come on, let's take the lift. That's what it's there for. There's no point in wearing ourselves out when we need all our energies for the investigation.'

Although Rafferty, a smoker from the age of thirteen, had, this time, managed to remain off cigarettes for some months, his body seemed to have gained no discernible benefit; for he still became puffed if he climbed more than one flight of stairs. He was half-tempted to start smoking again.

As Llewellyn retraced his steps and joined Rafferty in the apartments' fair-sized lift, he sniffed the air and commented, 'You're still off the cigarettes, I take it?'

Rafferty nodded and pressed the button for the third floor. 'You're doing well. I know it's not easy.'

Rafferty's smile was more a half-grimace. The clean-living Llewellyn, of course, had never smoked, so how did he know how hard or easy it was to give up the habit of two-thirds of a lifetime?

'I know there are one or two backsliders at the station who insist that they've still given up,' Llewellyn confided. 'They don't seem to realize the smell of stale smoke from their clothes is a giveaway that they've started smoking again on the sly.'

Rafferty, not entirely convinced that he would get to the end of this investigation without being numbered amongst the backsliders, had his excuse ready, just in case. 'Abra's started smoking in the flat again. She said she's fed up having to go outside on the balcony every time she wants to smoke.'

To give Abra her due, she had kept up this self-imposed banishment for two months. 'I thought she might keep it up, but she's hasn't. It's tough, Dafyd, to continue not smoking when you live with a smoker.'

Abra was Rafferty's girlfriend. Llewellyn, Abra's cousin, had introduced them in April, some two months' ago. She and Rafferty had jelled at the very first meeting.

Llewellyn gave him a sideways look from his knowing dark eyes as the lift doors opened with a groan surprising in such a plush block and they emerged on the top floor.

'Is that the sound of you getting your excuses ready?' he asked as if he had read Rafferty's mind.

'Certainly not,' Rafferty indignantly replied.

He consulted his list and marched purposefully forward. 'Here's Mr Oliver's apartment. Number 3C.'

He rapped on the door, loudly enough to block any more attempts by his sergeant at reading his mind and possible intentions.

* * *

Although Hal Oliver, at seventy-five, had a face as cadaverous as Mick Jagger's and a neck as ropey as a yacht's equipment locker, he still had a rake-hell's attraction about him, accentuated by the thick white hair, which flowed, with a cavalier dash, around his ropey neck.

His trousers were creased, attesting to the fact that currently there was no woman in his life. But for all his creased trousers and neck, for all the cadaverous folds of flesh, the confidence good looks brought was still in evidence. It was there in the bold bright-blue gaze and the repose of his hands, which lay at ease on the arms of his chair as they questioned him.

When he led them into his small apartment, Rafferty had noted Hal Oliver walked with that upright, slow-paced slight swagger of a confident man at ease with himself.

Oliver's apartment had as rakish and lived-in an air as did the man himself. For all that he had only lived there for a short time he had already put his stamp on it. There was a huge chestnut-brown leather settee in front of the fireplace with a smaller one at right angles to it. Several battered leather trunks lined the walls and, above the trunks, hung many photographs of foreign parts, with Hal Oliver at various ages and with assorted attractive young women featuring in most of them.

After he had explained the recent tragic events, Rafferty said, 'I understand you were friendly with Mrs Mortimer? Even gave her flowers – red roses.'

Hal Oliver gave a rueful laugh. 'These old biddies don't miss much, do they?' he commented. 'Though *trying* to be friendly would be a more accurate description, Inspector,' he corrected. 'I liked her, for all that most of the other residents said they found her standoffish. Standoffishness is something I regard as a challenge. Besides, I think I'm right when I claim we share similar interests. Clara . . .' He paused, then as if belatedly realizing such a show of intimacy in front of the police was unwise, he corrected himself and became more formal. 'Mrs Mortimer – was a reserved woman.'

His blue eyes sparkling, Oliver flashed his devil-may-care smile. 'You could say the flowers I bought were merely a supplicant's offering, designed to knock a brick or two out of the wall she seems – seemed – to have built around herself.'

'I understand you've only recently moved to this apartment block,' Rafferty said. 'Did your friendship with Mrs Mortimer only start when you moved here?'

Hal Oliver nodded, then added enigmatically, 'Though, in a way, you could say we've known one another for years. I mean in another life, of course. I was just beginning to make Clara – Mrs Mortimer – appreciate that fact. Now . . .' He broke off, then made an expansive gesture with hands in which the veins stood out prominently. 'Well, you know the rest.'

After they had confirmation that he had been away from home at the time of Clara Mortimer's death and could give them no information, once he had supplied them with an alibi, they left.

'Rum character,' Rafferty commented as they walked down the stairs and stood chatting at the entrance. 'Did you notice he didn't seem as shocked as might be expected when we told him what had happened to Mrs Mortimer?'

Llewellyn nodded. 'Though Mr Oliver's appearance gives the impression he's knocked around the world a bit and is pretty much inured to shock.'

'He certainly seems to have lived a full life and seen the world. His photo collection makes Amelia Frobisher's look that of a lonely stay-at-home for all her determination to convince visitors to the contrary. Anyway,' he said as he reached his car, 'let's get back to the factory. We still have the rest of the reports to read before we can pack it in for the evening. Tomorrow, I shall want to speak to Clara Mortimer's old neighbour, Mary Soames, and see what she can tell us about Mrs Mortimer's family.

'I'll also want to speak to all the residents myself as soon as possible. They may recall something after a night's sleep. Not forgetting Mrs Mortimer's loving daughter and her boyfriend. I want to learn more about the recent row he had with the victim. If the row was about money, as seems possible to judge from the pair's circumstances, it's not difficult to suspect Jane Ogilvie might have been encouraged to ensure she got her inheritance early. Although she denied that she had keys to her mother's home, I noticed a set of keys hanging on a hook in their hall. The keys to the entrance door and to the individual apartments are very distinctive. I wonder why she should choose to lie about it?'

'Could be nothing – simply that she guessed we would learn of the argument Jesmond had with her mother and thought it better to err on the side of caution—'

Llewellyn was interrupted by the trilling of his mobile phone.

'That was Beard,' Llewellyn said five minutes later when he'd returned his mobile to his jacket pocket. 'He did the computer checks you asked for. He discovered that both Jane Ogilvie and Jesmond have criminal records for drug abuse and assault. So – going back to the keys – it's possible Mrs Ogilvie suspects her boyfriend's involved in her mother's death and decided to protect him.'

Rafferty nodded thoughtfully. 'That's something I shall certainly question her about tomorrow.'

Llewellyn's checks had also revealed that Jesmond's latest fine had been for a drunk and disorderly conviction, the latest of several, during which he had assaulted Jane. Their records indicated that both had ready tempers and were prone to violence.

'But before we question the pair again, we'll see this Mary Soames; she might provide us with some valuable leverage, especially as she seems to have known the victim for some years.'

With the hopeful thought that the morrow might bring the case to an all too squalid and predictable conclusion, Rafferty got in his car and returned to the station, with Llewellyn, in his own car, falling in behind.

It was an hour and a half later before they had got abreast of the remaining reports. Rafferty bade Llewellyn good night and headed for the hospital to offer his niece the belated congratulations or condolences the intrusion of that morning's murder had delayed.

He knew his new love, Abra, would be there. He hoped she would be in a more reasonable frame of mind than she had been on the previous evening when she had told Rafferty her news.

Even now, Rafferty felt shocked that Abra could have brought the possibility of turmoil into both their lives with such banal words. He hadn't even understood what she was saying at first . . .

'Joe. What do you feel about getting two for the price of one?'

Rafferty, immersed in the newspaper, finally relaxing after the demands of work, had raised his eyes from the newsprint. 'What's that, light of my life? Some special offer at the supermarket?'

'Not quite, no. I'm not talking about buying a packet of cornflakes and getting a second one free. I'm talking about you and me and a possible addition to our numbers.'

Rafferty had blanched as her meaning had sunk in. His fingers developed a death grip on his newspaper. It was now June; they'd only met in April. Rafferty had never thought that Abra might be the sort of girl to become obsessed by babies. What was it she had said when they had first met? When he had remarked that Llewellyn, her cousin, had told him that her name meant 'Mother of Multitudes' and asked her if she thought she might be, her reply had been 'Not bloody likely!'

Now, he was so astonished to discover she had done a complete about turn that he could find nothing to say. The seconds lengthened, became a strained half minute. Then Abra broke the silence.

'Your enthusiasm overwhelms me.'

Her words didn't auger well for the pleasant, relaxed evening Rafferty had promised himself.

Abra's face became as set as a jelly at his continuing shocked silence. But it freed up sufficiently for her to observe, 'So, I guess I can take it that you don't want our child.'

Belatedly becoming aware that the ice beneath his feet was thin and that he was in imminent danger of sinking up to his neck in previously unchartered waters, Rafferty quickly riposted, 'I didn't say that.'

Like most bombshells, Abra's had come without warning. *Was* she pregnant? Or only telling him that she'd like to be? He relaxed a bit when he realized she couldn't be pregnant. Hadn't they always used contraception?

Tentatively, he asked, 'Can we just backtrack a little and establish some facts? *Are* you pregnant?'

Abra frowned. Said, 'Yes . . . no . . . maybe,' before she burst in to tears.

This alarmed Rafferty even more. After experiencing the various pregnancies of three younger sisters and recently that of his niece, Gemma, he recognized the signs of upside-down hormones only too well.

Instinctively, while he frantically sought for soothing words, he dropped his newspaper and gathered Abra in his arms. After a little, when her tears had subsided to hiccups and sniffs, he said, 'I thought you were on the pill? So how . . . ?'

'I was. But you remember that gastric upset I had around six weeks ago?'

Above her head, Rafferty gave a wary nod.

'It must have happened just after, when we celebrated

my recovery. I never gave it a thought at the time, but I must have sicked up the contraceptive pill each time I heaved. I heaved quite a lot if you remember?'

Rafferty did remember. Abra's gastric upset had been worryingly violent. That was why their celebration of her recovery had been so joyous and abandoned.

His mind in turmoil, he said, 'Pregnancy's pretty unlikely, though, isn't it? We only celebrated the once, after all.'

Abra sniffed again. 'Didn't they teach you any biology at that repressive Catholic school you went to? Believe me, once *is* enough.'

He knew that. Of course he did. Only he felt it *shouldn't* be enough. It seemed such a cheap trick of the Almighty, after one thoughtless act to land them with the prospect of night shrieks, nappies and a twenty-year, hundred-grand-plus bill. But cheap tricks from the Almighty were something of a feature in Rafferty's life.

He took heart from what Abra had said earlier. 'You don't sound too sure whether you're pregnant or not. If it was me I'd want to know for certain if I was about to become a parent.'

All too belatedly, when Abra's only response was more tears, Rafferty tried to provide some solace. 'Well, I suppose it's not the end of the world if you *are* pregnant.' Even to his own ears his reassurance sounded desperately hollow. So he wasn't surprised when Abra wrenched herself out of his arms and rounded on him.

'You're saying you don't want to be a parent, aren't you? At least tell me the truth. I think I'm entitled to that much.'

Rafferty prevaricated. 'Well, it's true that I hadn't thought of becoming a father so soon in our relationship. But if you *are* pregnant, I'm sure I'll get used to the idea. So, tell me – are you?'

Abra sniffed again. She snatched a tissue from a box on the coffee table and blew her nose so vehemently that its little tip turned pink. 'I told you. I don't know. And with you being so negative about it, I'm not sure I want to. Maybe it's better if we both have time to adjust to the possibility before we find out for certain.'

'Ignorance isn't necessarily bliss, Abs,' he said. 'I know,' he suggested with a jolly, encouraging air, 'why don't we go to the late-night chemist and buy a pregnancy testing kit?'

She must have sensed his fear at the possibility of looming parental responsibility for she reacted to his sensible idea as if he was patronizing her and immediately turned mulish.

'No. I said I don't want to know and now I'm sure of it. You don't want our baby – if we're having one – do you? Admit it.'

Rafferty opened his mouth then closed it again. And though after a few tense moments, he found words and courage to try to discuss it again, he discovered he was too late. Abra refused to say any more on the subject.

It was their first row. If this simmering brew of questions with no answers could even properly be called a row. Whether it was or not, it was also the first night they went to bed and clung determinedly to opposite edges of the double divan. An uncomfortable night was had by the two – or possibly the three – of them.

When Rafferty got to the hospital, he found Abra already there.

Gemma, his niece, looked red-eyed and tearful. No doubt she was quailing at the prospect of being responsible for a new baby. Although it was a long time since he had been sixteen, it was a feeling Rafferty could empathize with; he was quailing at the possibility himself.

He kissed them both, but Abra determinedly averted her lips, presented her cheek for a peck and immediately drew back, so Rafferty knew he was still in the doghouse.

He wondered whether Abra had been discussing him with Gemma because although they'd been chatting readily enough when he walked through the door to the small ward, their conversation had quickly faded after his arrival.

He tried his uncle's duty of jollying Gemma along with the lie, 'You look better than you did this morning, sweetheart. Your mum said they'll let you out tomorrow, you and your little bundle.'

He was nonplussed when his innocent comment prompted Gemma to burst into tears.

'Honestly, Joseph.' Stiff-necked, Abra reproved him. 'If you can't say anything helpful, don't you think it would be better to say nothing at all?'

Through her sobs as Abra tried to comfort her and make up for her clumsy uncle, Gemma said, 'You make it sound like I'm being let out of prison – only . . . only it's a prison I'm *going* to and for the rest of my life. It's all right for you, Uncle Joe, you haven't got to face the prospect of having the next twenty-odd years of your life all laid out, like I have.'

I wouldn't bet on it, kiddo, was Rafferty's thought as he glanced at Abra's set face.

Faced with the twin tasks of trying to console Gemma and convey to Abra that he was sure he'd *love* the idea of parenthood once he got use to it, Rafferty remarked, 'Oh, I don't know, sweet-pea. These things naturally take time to adjust to. I don't think you'll find it as difficult as you fear. I bet you'll feel differently in a week when you've got the little tyke home and settled in and he's given you his first burpy smile.'

For some reason, his words of comfort brought a further gush of tears from Gemma.

Now what have I said? he asked himself.

Once again, he didn't have to remain in ignorance for long.

Abra gave him a withering look and told him in a whispered aside, 'Gemma's having trouble breastfeeding.'

'It's so *gross*,' Gemma wailed. 'And it *hurts*. Why did no one tell me it would hurt when they were so busy explaining how good it would be for *him*? What about me? What about what's best for me?'

Rafferty, about to light-heartedly remark that he didn't think breastfeeding had yet become compulsory, thought better of it.

Thankfully, just then, the Rafferty family matriarch, his ma, Kitty, arrived with his sister, Maggie, and he was able to retreat to his natural role among this Sisterhood – that of the villainous male, one of the species who had brought about Gemma's trouble in the first place.

Even his ma scolded him when Abra explained the reason for Gemma's freshly tear-streaked face.

'Now, Joseph, you're not to go upsetting the poor girl any more.' Kitty Rafferty's laser-gaze took a swift inventory of the gifts of flowers and tiny garments displayed on the bedside table next to Gemma each with the gift tag of the giver still attached. 'I see you didn't even think to bring your niece and your great-nephew a little gift.'

Rafferty, guilty as charged and forced to admit to yet another failing, could only watch in shamed silence as his ma proceeded to empty her own selection of 'little gifts' on to the bed.

Soon, the soiled lemon duvet cover was buried beneath romper suits in modern, multicoloured hues, enough Babygros to indicate Mothercare might be a good future investment and sufficient rattles to equip the loudest of Manchester United's many supporters. She had even thought to buy the new mother something to cheer her up; tickets for some boy band's concert for the following week. This last brought a miraculous stemming to Gemma's tears. All at once she looked what she was: a teenager in the first flush of infatuation.

It gave Rafferty an inkling of how he could redeem himself with Abra, Gemma and the rest of the females in his life. He snatched a glance at the date on the concert tickets and resolved to offer to baby-sit. It wouldn't be easy. Not only was he just at the beginning of another murder case, but he reckoned he would have to arm-wrestle his ma, Mrs Newson, Maggie and his other sisters and nieces for the privilege.

Somehow, Rafferty got through the rest of the hospital visit without further upsets. But Abra, when he brought the subject up again as they drove home, still refused to take a pregnancy test.

'But *why* won't you?' Rafferty asked again. 'I know you said—'

'I know what I said. I also know what *you* said. I've thought of little else. Your rejection of our baby went round and round in my head all last night.'

'I *haven't* rejected it,' Rafferty insisted. 'But,' yet again he pointed out, not unreasonably he thought, 'we still don't even know for certain if we *are* having a baby.'

'No. And as I said, I think it's best if it stays that way. At least till I'm past the period for the legal termination I suspect you'll be angling for.'

'That's unfair, Abra. I haven't even mentioned the possibility of you having a termination.'

'No. But I bet you've *thought* it though, haven't you?'

Even though he hadn't given a thought to abortion, in all honesty he had to admit to himself that this might be because he hadn't had time for such thoughts. Given time, such a possibility might well have crossed his mind.

It was unfortunate that, by this time, they had reached Rafferty's flat and turned all the lights on. Because after taking one look at his face – which had never guarded his real feelings too well – Abra shrieked, 'You, you *pig!*' at him, turned on her heel, her long, lustrous plait of hair swinging behind her, and stormed out, back to her own flat, without another word.

It was yet another first. Abra had moved into his flat three weeks after they had met and – apart from the demands of work – they hadn't spent a night apart since.

Their little difference was beginning to set records at an alarming rate. The previous night spent at opposite sides of the bed had been bad enough, but this was ten times worse. The situation was beginning to accelerate away from him, Rafferty realized; soon they could be past the point of no return. The ridiculous part was that he wasn't even sure he was that set against becoming a father.

Grimly, Rafferty faced the possibility that he might be about to lose Abra. This was sobering. Because he'd only just found her . . .

It was certainly too sobering a thought to face without alcohol, he thought, as he reached for the bottle of Jameson's and poured himself a generous measure.

Five

After a night spent brooding, wondering what to do for the best, bleary-eyed, Rafferty left for the station. He had tried to contact Abra several times the previous evening, but she had left her answerphone switched on and in spite of his desperate pleading, she had chosen to take none of his calls.

Somehow, he knew he would have to find time during a busy day of interviews to go round to her flat. At least she should be there, as he knew she'd taken this week as a holiday from her job in order to do some long overdue spring cleaning.

Rafferty, beginning to worry that he'd be spring-cleaned out of Abra's life along with the dust and cobwebs, had reason to regret his shocked response to her news. But how had she expected him to react? He wasn't far off forty, already more than halfway through the biblical three score years and ten. At his age he should be thinking of putting more money into his pension, not taking on – if the newspapers were to be believed about the costs of modern child-rearing – what sounded like a chunk of the National Debt.

His appalled reaction had been exacerbated by memories of another pregnancy – that of his late wife, Angie. Then, too, failed contraception had brought about an unplanned pregnancy, followed by a shotgun wedding and years of unhappiness and acrimony; years not even relieved by the consolation of a bouncing baby who grew into a loved child as Angie had miscarried shortly after the wedding.

Rafferty felt certain that if Abra *did* turn out to be pregnant that the outcome wouldn't be anything like his previous experience. For one thing – and in spite of this recent turmoil – he believed he and Abra were soulmates in a way that he and Angie had never been. If only he could get over the bad memories, he might come round to the idea of fatherhood. He would have to, he acknowledged, as he was aware that if he didn't he might lose Abra altogether.

But for now, he knew he must put to one side all such thoughts and get on with the murder investigation.

Fortunately, they didn't even have to trace Mary Soames. She came forward immediately she read of Clara Mortimer's brutal murder in the morning's *Elmhurst Echo*.

Mary Soames it seemed, like her late friend, Mrs Mortimer, was an early riser, for she had already rung the station and arranged for them to call to see her by the time Rafferty arrived at work.

As Rita Atkins had said, Mrs Soames lived in the southern outskirts of Elmhurst in a spacious, Georgian-style detached house enclosed within what looked to be about an acre of land.

As Rafferty and Llewellyn drew up outside the front door and parked on a short gravelled drive lined with what looked like hand-thrown tubs filled with deliciously scented pinks and butterfly lavender, Rafferty caught a glimpse of the tall chimney pots of another, much older house through the trees. He wondered if that had been where Clara Mortimer had previously lived. Mary Soames confirmed it when she opened the door.

Although elderly like Clara Mortimer, the two women appeared on the surface to have little else in common. Mary Soames was short and round, with a fresh, pleasant face that exuded interest in everything around her. She had certainly noticed Rafferty's drawing in of a deep, pink-scented breath, because she insisted on pulling some up by the roots to give to him.

'Clara inherited the Little Dower House from her parents,' she told them in response to Rafferty's question. 'She sold The Manor, the original family home, shortly after she inherited it. Understandable, I suppose, as the upkeep was crippling. But even the Dower House is a sizeable property, much too big for her, she said, and it was too far to town. We're not on a bus route here and Clara never learned to drive. She sold it in the new year.' Softly, she added, 'I think the memories that came with the house were another factor.'

'Memories?' Rafferty queried.

'Her marriage broke up while she was living there.' Mary Soames gave them a warm smile. 'But let's not stand gossiping on the doorstep like a couple of fishwives, Inspector. If you've come to learn about poor Clara's life, you might as well do it in comfort. Come in.'

Mrs Soames led them through a large, bright hallway to a homely living room, scattered with evidence of many interests; books of poetry jostled for space with easels and watercolour paints. The black ink of calligraphy nestled dangerously close to delicate cobwebs of embroidery. Dust motes from tables that clearly received only a desultory polish danced in the shaft of sunlight beaming in through the surprisingly clean windows.

Mary Soames's hairpins and jewellery also managed to scatter themselves around the room. Her thick white hair was screwed into an untidy bun and every time she moved her head, one more hairpin would fly out and another hank of hair would fall on to her neck. She jabbed it back with another pin taken from the capacious pocket of the paint-spattered blue smock, but in the process managed to send one of her pearl studs flying from her ear, which the well-mannered Llewellyn retrieved.

But thankfully, while Mary Soames might not appear to

have control over her hair or her jewellery, and while her living room might be a chaotic riot of hobbies, her control over her memory turned out to be excellent.

Over tea and biscuits, which she fetched on a tray from the kitchen after removing skeins of wool and a fat tabby cat from the armchairs so they could sit down, she told them more about Clara Mortimer's life.

'Clara could be a bit rigid, I suppose. I've known her since she was a girl; we were at school together and I know she was very strictly brought up. Her family were well to do and they instilled in her the "right" way to behave. Her rigid upbringing made her incapable of swaying with passing social mores. I imagine that's why, when her daughter told her she was getting divorced, she reacted so strongly.

'There had never been a divorce in the family, you see,' Mary Soames explained. 'Clara hadn't even considered getting a divorce when her husband left her. Harry Mortimer has always been a bit of a rogue and is completely unreliable, but he can turn on the charm when it suits him – more's the pity for poor Clara. I often think she would have had a happier life if she had never met him.

'Clara's parents always maintained she had married beneath her. I have to say I agreed with them. With all his love affairs and his careless fathering of other women's children he broke Clara's heart. I felt that Harry leaving her was the best thing that could happen to Clara.'

She leant forward, picked up a photo from the cluttered side table and handed it to Rafferty.

'That's Harry Mortimer,' she said. 'It was taken on their wedding day.'

Rafferty wondered why she should trouble to show him a picture of Clara Mortimer's late husband since death had removed him as a possible suspect, but for politeness's sake, he leaned forward and took it, anyway.

The strapping, handsome man in the photo had the

mischievous, dancing eyes and ready grin that indicated he would be a handful, thought Rafferty. Beside him, Clara looked slim and demure in a sheath-style ivory dress and short, diaphanous veil. On closer inspection, although the demure expression remained, there was no mistaking the look of triumph in her eye. It proclaimed that having caught her man, she had proved you could have your cake and eat it.

Given what Mary Soames had said about the marriage, Rafferty couldn't help but wonder how long it had taken for disillusionment to set in and for Clara to realize that, as a husband, Harry Mortimer wasn't, after all, such a great prize.

Once Llewellyn, too, had glanced at the picture, Rafferty handed it back.

Mrs Soames returned the photo to the table and picked up her tea. It was in a thick eartheware mug rather than the exquisite and almost translucent china cups in Clara Mortimer's kitchen. But, given the way Mary Soames's possessions seemed to scatter about her, it was probably just as well she favoured more workmanlike drinking vessels.

'Clara was ashamed that it should be *her* daughter who was the family's first divorcée, especially after the trauma she felt when Jane fell pregnant with Charles, her eldest.'

Rafferty, who had forgotten to make enquiries about the identity of the young man in RAF uniform in the faded sepia photo in Clara Mortimer's apartment, was thankful when Mrs Soames confirmed that the photo *was* that of Mrs Mortimer's elder brother, another Charles.

'Clara adored him. He died in the war, but he lived long enough to father two children who are both doing well, I believe, though since they emigrated to New Zealand with their mother, I've rather lost touch.

'I was pleased, for Clara's sake, when Jane and James Ogilvie married. I suppose I might have known it wouldn't last. Jane really went off the rails after that. Awful to say, perhaps, but maybe it was for the best that she miscarried several times after the marriage split. She was living a very rackety life at the time, so I imagine the babies stood a good chance of being damaged in some way.'

'Talking about Mrs Ogilvie's children,' Rafferty said. 'For purposes of elimination, I need to find out the names and addresses of their fathers, but I didn't feel I could ask Mrs Ogilvie yesterday after breaking the news about her mother's murder. Did you know them? Or know their current whereabouts?'

'I met all three, but the only one I knew reasonably well was James Ogilvie. As for where they might be living now . . .' She shrugged. 'I doubt if Jane herself knows as she's never been a great one for keeping in touch.

'I would imagine Hakim's father, Jamil Abdullah, has probably long since returned to Egypt; he was only here on a student visa and made no secret of the fact that his long-term commitment was to his homeland rather than Jane.

'As for Aurora's father – Earl Ray, he called himself, though I believe he also used several other names – he was a bad lot, into buying and selling drugs. He's more than likely dead by now. I don't mind admitting I was glad when he cleared out of Jane's life. He wasn't a good influence on the children. Certainly neither of these men was what I would call good father material.

'Unfortunately, with Jane, that's par for the course. She had always been something of a trial to poor Clara. Whatever Clara asked her to do, Jane did the opposite. Anyway, after their disagreement about the divorce, things rather went downhill. Sometimes I swear that Jane behaved the way she did just to upset her mother. After all, she can't *want* to have had all of her children conceived with different fathers. Even though she's only a year off forty, Jane is still going through her rebellious teens in her head. The trouble is, Clara and her daughter never got on. Jane is too much like her father, but didn't inherit his charm. And then, I don't think Jane ever got over her father leaving. She thought Harry Mortimer was the sun, the moon and the stars.'

'And what about James Ogilvie? Does he keep in touch with his son?'

Mrs Soames shrugged. 'As to that, I wouldn't know. I haven't set eyes on young Charles for years.' She smiled. 'I rather think, in Jane's mind I was lumped together with her mother and dismissed as another straight-laced old woman. She certainly never encouraged her children to visit me.'

Unsurprised, Rafferty nodded at this. 'Tell me,' he said. 'Do you know if Mrs Mortimer made a will?'

Mary Soames shook her head. 'I'm afraid not, though I doubt it. Clara always put off writing a will. But you could check with her solicitors – Parkes, Parkes and Witherspoon in East Street.'

While Rafferty made a note of this information, Mary Soames continued. 'Clara was old-fashioned about a number of things. She didn't deem husbands or money suitable subjects for conversation. For Clara, her money and her husband were subjects only suitably discussed with the Almighty. She tolerated my impertinence – just – because she always thought of me as being something of a bohemian.'

Mary Soames laughed. It was a rich laugh, full of pleasure in life. 'Clara could be unimaginative and often looked no further than the surface of things. No doubt that's how she ended up marrying Harry Mortimer. I'm no more a bohemian than my vicar father. All I am is a lazy housewife with an interest in the arts.'

Her bright eyes twinkled at them over her mug. 'Of course, with Clara, I played up to the bohemian tag for all I was worth. I thought it a better label than that of domestic slut, which would be more accurate. Sometimes, when my untidy house got too much for her, Clara would send over her cleaning lady and stump up the cost. She didn't do it often, though. I always had the feeling that Clara rather liked my disordered house after the controlled environment of her own. I suspect my home was the one place Clara allowed herself to let her hair down a little.'

Mary Soames sighed. 'Poor Clara. In many ways, she had a sad life. I always hoped she'd learn to loosen up as she got older. Now, she'll never get the chance to become the disreputable old lady I thought she had it in her to be. I suppose her natural effervescence was repressed for too long.'

It was only as they were about to leave, Rafferty with the carrier bag of pinks wrapped in wet newspaper that were destined for his ma's garden, that curiosity impelled him to question Mrs Soames further.

'Since I understand from Mrs Ogilvie that Clara's husband died some years ago, I wondered—' he began only to be interrupted.

'Oh no, Inspector.' Mary Soames shook her head. Another hairpin flew off. 'That's not right at all. I don't know why Jane should tell you such nonsense. Harry Mortimer's not dead at all.'

Six

Mary Soames's revelation shook Rafferty. It was only now he realized that all her references to Harry Mortimer had been in the present tense. He had just assumed she had not learned of his death. Stupid really, she had been in regular contact with Clara Mortimer, who might have been relied upon to know if the father of her only child was still alive or not.

Having shaken them once, Mrs Soames proceeded to shake them a second time.

'Far from being dead,' Mary Soames explained, 'Clara told me Harry Mortimer had actually moved into one of the cheaper apartments in her block and was attempting to woo her all over again. Only for some reason he calls himself Hal Oliver.

'I can only presume he's trying to escape some creditors. Or perhaps the Child Support Agency managed to catch up with him at last. It's common knowledge that he's left a trail of illegitimate children behind him. Hard to believe at his age, I know, but I heard that he only fathered the last one two years ago.'

Rafferty was annoyed with himself that he had yet to get around to checking what Jane Ogilvie had told him. The fact that he had had no reason to doubt what she said was insufficient excuse; especially as she had now proved herself as proficient a liar as her father.

Still, he couldn't allow himself to become excited at these latest revelations; they had investigated the alibi Hal Oliver had given them and DC Lilley, whom he had assigned the job, had confirmed it had checked out. Hal Oliver – or Harry Mortimer as it now turned out was his true identity – had told them he had stayed overnight with a male friend in central London and had shared breakfast with his friend on the morning of Mrs Mortimer's murder. Afterwards, Lilley said Hal Oliver's friend, Mike Brown, had told him Hal had gone off to complete some urgent and long overdue errands before he had caught the train back to Elmhurst.

Lilley, whom Rafferty had always found an intelligent and entirely competent detective, had taken the trouble to check this story with the porter at Mr Brown's apartment block. The porter had confirmed what Oliver/Mortimer and his friend had said.

Yet now, Rafferty began to have serious doubts. Was it possible that Mike Brown, the porter and Oliver/Mortimer himself had all colluded in the lie and he hadn't stayed overnight with his friend in London at all? With Clara Mortimer dead it certainly looked to be a possibility.

Rafferty gave his head a tiny shake and tuned back in to what Mary Soames was saying.

'Harry always did carry fatherhood too lightly for Jane to turn out anything but needy. I often think her father, rather than her mother, was the cause of most of her problems.'

Rafferty said, 'Tell me, what did Mrs Mortimer think of these renewed attentions from her estranged husband?'

'You know, I suspect she was rather tickled. She still loved him, you see, in spite of everything. She was always very fastidious about her appearance, but she became even more so. She had her hair styled twice a week instead of her usual once and treated herself to some tailor-made suits and dresses. She even bought an up-to-the-minute computer, I presume so that if any of Harry's numerous offspring should happen to call, they would be able to play their computer games. Harry, naturally, hadn't even thought of providing such an amusement himself.'

They all pondered this for a few moments. Then Rafferty ventured another question. 'Did you think it would have been a good idea for Mrs Mortimer to get back with her husband?'

Mary Soames didn't require any more than a second to consider the question. 'No, not at all,' was her immediate response. 'Harry Mortimer was always bad news as far as Clara was concerned. She was the only one who couldn't see it.'

She sighed and added, 'But there, she was always foolish over that man, no matter how sensible she was in every other area. Harry had cheated on her I don't know how many times, sponged off her quite shamelessly and finally left her to bring up their child on her own. I thought allowing him back into her life was the worst possible thing for her. We nearly had a falling out over it, actually, especially when I told her it would end in tears.'

She paused to add poignantly, 'And now it has. Though I never thought it would come to this.'

Mary Soames had given them a lot to think about, particularly her last enigmatic comment and its implication that she thought Clara Mortimer's estranged husband could have had something to do with her death.

It was certainly suspicious that, a mere two weeks before her murder, he should have moved into the same apartment block as his estranged wife.

With so much to think about, Rafferty was happy to let Llewellyn drive; his slower style of locomotion would, he thought, enable him to turn these latest discoveries over in his mind and decide how best to approach the questioning of Harry Mortimer aka Hal Oliver and his alibi-producing friend.

'Why would Jane Ogilvie tell us her father was dead?' he asked Llewellyn as the latter negotiated his careful way round the roundabout that led them back to Priory Way. 'She must have known we'd find out the truth.'

'Mrs Ogilvie struck me as an impetuous person,' Llewellyn remarked, with a moue of distaste for such an undesirable character trait. 'One who acts first and thinks afterwards, if at all.'

She was in good company, thought Rafferty wryly. He had ever been impetuous. He bit the bullet and commented, 'Yes, that's my opinion, too.' Takes one to know one, he thought. 'You've only got to consider her careless approach to the responsibilities of parenthood.'

The words were barely out of his mouth before his conscience struck him a metaphorical rap over the knuckles. Judge not – lest ye yourself be judged, it said. For once, he had no quick, conscience-silencing riposte.

Llewellyn nodded. 'Harry Mortimer sounds to me to be the kind of charming rogue of a father that little girls adore, so I presume Jane Ogilvie still feels some affection for him and wanted to protect him. Presumably, she was scared we would think him the obvious suspect.'

Damn right, was Rafferty's natural response. But once again he kept his thought to himself.

Llewellyn continued. 'Especially given that Mortimer's estranged wife was a fairly wealthy woman and he had so conveniently moved into the same block.'

'It's certainly an interesting pointer that she should lie for him so automatically. And it *was* automatic,' he told Llewellyn when he recalled that his sergeant hadn't witnessed Jane Ogilvie's lie. 'She didn't even pause for thought. It strikes me it was something she was used to doing; presumably when one of his discarded mistresses was trying to track him down. But it's even more interesting that she should feel the need to lie about him to *us* as well as raging mistresses. It gives us another indication as to the man's character should we need one after listening to what Mrs Soames had to say about him.'

Rafferty reached forward. 'I'll get on to the station and get Lilley to again check out Mortimer's friend, Mike

Brown, and the alibi he supplied. If Mortimer *was* still at this Brown's apartment at the time Clara Mortimer died someone else apart from a possibly bribable porter may have seen him coming and going. While I'm at it, I'll get him to check Mortimer out under *both* his names.'

Much to his surprise, a couple of minutes later, DC Jonathon Lilley came back with the news that Harry Mortimer had no criminal convictions under either his own name or his adopted name.

'Perhaps he has a third name he uses for criminal activities,' was Rafferty's comment as he replaced the speaker-mike.

Rafferty began to regret handing the car keys to Llewellyn. The late Mrs Mortimer's estranged, but very much alive husband, sounded an interesting prospect – more so given that they had so far failed to find the dead woman's will. If no will turned up at the solicitors that Mrs Soames had mentioned, then Harry Mortimer could be in line for a substantial inheritance under the intestacy laws.

That possibility brought a number of questions to mind. Not least why Mortimer had chosen to relocate himself to the same apartment block as the victim? So he could again woo the woman he had already rejected once, as Mary Soames claimed?

It seemed unlikely. Somehow, Rafferty doubted that wooing his estranged wife had been high on Harry Mortimer's agenda.

So what had been?

The more he thought about it, the more Rafferty regretted not knowing Harry Mortimer was very much alive when they had interviewed Hal Oliver/Harry Mortimer first time round. The delay would have given him ample time to come up with more plausible lies to account for the concealment of his identity and his recent house move to the apartment block of his estranged wife. What was it the Bible said about liars?

Rafferty racked his brains as they waited at the zebra crossing for a gaggle of schoolchildren to cross the road. It was only when Llewellyn had started up again that, as clear as clear, in his head echoed the voice of Miss Robson, his old junior school religious teacher. How could he have forgotten, especially when she had so frequently quoted it about *him*?

'There is no truth in him. When he speaketh a lie, he speaketh of his own: for he is a liar, and the father of it.'

The father of it – and maybe the *friend* of it also, as like sought like. Given that Harry Mortimer had already proven himself a more than proficient liar, it seemed an odds on possibility that his obliging friend, Mike Brown, was a man of the same ilk.

At that thought, Rafferty's foot pressed a non-existent accelerator pedal to the floor in his eagerness – now he was armed with excellent ammunition – to question Mortimer again.

As Hal Oliver-Mortimer let them in, Rafferty again noted the confident way he walked. This was not a man bowed by age or sin, was Rafferty's firm opinion. All his years and his sins looked lightly borne. Guilt for all the father-less children that Mary Soames mentioned he had left in his wake had left few tracks on his forehead. In fact, unlike the rest of his face, his forehead was strangely unmarked by the passage of time or sin: those marks, those sins, had been borne by others.

Blithely must he have passed through his life and the lives of others, Rafferty thought, not even noticing the damage he left behind him. The man might be a wraith – a spirit who touched the lives of many, but who was himself untouched.

Rafferty wasn't sure whether to feel sad at the shallow emptiness of Harry Mortimer's life or be impressed by how successfully he had evaded what should have been his many responsibilities. Clearly, he had the 'bugger you, I'm all right' outlook, which a younger Rafferty would probably have admired.

But now, as the older Rafferty thought of young Gemma and the countless Gemmas males like Mortimer left in their roués' wakes, he felt only anger, an anger not lessened by his own guilty feelings about Abra, followed by an urgent desire to tell the man a few home truths. But the thought that similar home truths would find as ready a billet with him as with Mortimer made him restrain the impulse.

Besides, to be fair to the man, disarmingly, Mortimer admitted he had lied to them before they even began to question him; before they even had a chance to take the seats he so smilingly offered.

This ready admission that he had lied to them the previous day rather took the wind out of Rafferty's sails. This, together with his uncomfortable cocktail of feelings, caused him to launch straight in with questions.

'Why didn't you admit when we took your statement yesterday that you used to have another name and were the victim's estranged husband?'

'Why do you think?' Harry looked from Llewellyn to Rafferty and back again before he laughed and raised his arms in an expansive gesture as if inviting them to share the joke. 'It was panic pure and simple. When that young detective told me what had happened to Clara, I knew I needed to sort out an alibi and quickly. If I didn't I felt convinced you would have immediately marked me down as chief suspect.'

Rafferty sat back in the leather settee and folded his arms. Bluntly, he demanded, 'So why have you decided to tell us the truth about all this now? What's changed?'

Mortimer shrugged. 'The panic subsided. Also, I suppose I've had time to think. I'm not a complete fool. I knew you would certainly have discovered my relationship to Clara sooner or later – one of my grandchildren could easily have spilled the beans, so I thought it would be better if I told you myself.'

'Very sensible of you. So tell me Mr – should it be Oliver or Mortimer?'

'Mortimer, I think.' Like an emperor on his throne, Harry Mortimer lounged back in his leather armchair, crossed one leg over his knee, completely at ease and candidly confessed, 'I never really changed my name, not properly, anyway. It was just one of those things one does to ease one's passage through life, so to speak.'

He looked thoughtful for a moment. A spark of emotion – regret? – seemed to cross his face. 'Maybe it's time I faced up to my responsibilities. What is it that they say, Inspector? That it's never too late to do the decent thing?'

He fixed Rafferty with such a piercing, still vivid-blue gaze as he said this that Rafferty felt uncomfortably certain that, in him, Harry Mortimer, that previously nonchalant shrugger-off of responsibilities, thought he recognized a twin soul.

Whether his glib talk about 'responsibilities' meant anything or not, when Rafferty questioned him about his alibi Mortimer shrugged and admitted:

'That was another lie, I'm afraid. Please don't blame my friend. After I spoke to that young detective on my return here, I got straight on the phone to Mike and pressurized him. As I said, as soon as I learned about Clara's death. I knew how it would look to the police.'

'So where were you?'

'I was here, in Elmhurst. While my poor, dear, estranged Clara was being murdered, I was sharing a delightful picnic breakfast with my daughter and her eldest.'

'And they'll confirm this?

Mortimer nodded.

For the life of him, Rafferty couldn't see any reason to believe Mortimer *or* his daughter, because Mortimer had supplied this alternative alibi in as careless, nonchalant and take-it-or-leave-it a manner as the man presented himself. He certainly didn't seem concerned whether they believed him or not.

Had he killed his wife? Rafferty asked himself as Mortimer closed the door behind them. And was his manner the challenge to them to prove it?

Imperceptibly, Rafferty shook his head. The answer to this case couldn't be that simple – could it? But, that said, he found it easy enough to believe that Mortimer's family would lie for him; men like Mortimer had been getting foolish females to lie for them for centuries. It was, with such men, almost a reflex action.

Had Jane lied for him solely because telling lies was her habitual response when anyone questioned her about her father's doings?

Or, this time, was she aware that she had a definite need to lie for him?

Rafferty pondered the pros and cons and decided he didn't know which way to jump. But part of him couldn't quite manage to accept that this case might after all turn out to be nothing more than a simple domestic between a married couple who, having already failed to get on once, had failed a second time and with deadly effect.

But, if he was wrong, Rafferty suspected that proving it would be neither easy nor simple, especially given Harry Mortimer's carelessly insouciant countenance – a countenance that seemed, to Rafferty, to be issuing a challenge to them to prove he had murdered his wife.

Seven

Back in the car after getting Harry Mortimer's latest version of the truth, Rafferty grunted with annoyance. He'd forgotten all about DC Lilley, whom he had sent haring off to London on a wild-goose chase to re-interview Harry Mortimer's friend, Mike Brown.

There was little point in speaking to the man again, now that Mortimer had owned up that he had been in Elmhurst all the time.

Then he remembered something else he had forgotten. So far, they had had no joy in speaking to 'Fancy' Freddie Talbot; the man never seemed to be at home. But maybe this time they'd be lucky.

He directed Llewellyn to turn the car round and make for Talbot's address.

For once, Freddie Talbot was at home. He turned out to be quite a natty gent – hence the 'Fancy' moniker Rita Atkins had given him.

Freddie Talbot sported a red silk cravat and a walking stick topped with a round ball of what looked like solid silver but couldn't be if the rest of the flat was anything to go by. Talbot would surely have pawned it when it became clear that Amelia Frobisher had cast him off for good.

He used the walking stick more to emphasize points in his conversation than to help him get about after the fall he told them he had suffered earlier in the week.

Although, with his red silk cravat, jaunty pepper-and-salt moustache and silver-topped cane, he cut something of a dash, it was plain, as Rafferty had already deduced, that this dash didn't go deep.

Talbot's small flat looked shabby and uncared for. Talbot himself, with his attempts at sartorial elegance succeeded only in drawing attention to the fact that beneath the navy blazer that smelled faintly of mothballs, the collar of his shirt was threadbare.

'Keeping up appearances' was the expression that came to mind. How Talbot must rue the day he tried to catch Clara Mortimer's interest and managed only to lose that of Amelia Frobisher, who herself couldn't be short of the readies.

Now, thought Rafferty, 'Fancy' Freddie Talbot, with neither a bird in the hand nor one in the bush, didn't seem very fancy at all.

Talbot's pale-grey eyes were damp and although he – just – managed to keep up the jaunty front, it was clearly becoming more of an effort the longer they stayed.

'I understand you've known Amelia Frobisher for some years.' Rafferty finally got down to the questioning when Talbot's relentless flow of talk about 'poor, dear Clara' finally came to a halt.

Talbot sighed, noticeably his damp eyes dampened still further.

'I fear I've blotted my copybook there,' he artlessly confided. 'And although I know Amelia can be a very unforgiving woman, I'll love her to my dying breath. What am I to do?' he appealed to Rafferty. 'She's quite cut me off. I can't bear it and I so used to enjoy the outings she organized to the theatre and the occasional intimate little dinners she cooked.'

Rafferty couldn't decide whether it was Amelia or her 'little dinners' that Talbot missed the most.

Freddie Talbot looked hopefully at Rafferty. 'I say, would you be a good chap and put in a word for me?' With his cane, he gestured at his injured leg, which didn't, to Rafferty, seem to have much wrong with it and said, 'Make me out to be at death's door, if you think it would help.'

Talbot chewed anxiously at his moustache. 'Maybe that will bring her round. What do you think?'

Personally, Rafferty thought Freddie Talbot had as much hope of re-engaging the unforgiving eye and interest of Amelia Frobisher as he had of getting clan Mortimer-Ogilvie to all tell him the truth unvarnished. But as Talbot looked as if he might burst into tears if Rafferty told him that his hoped-for reconciliation with Miss Frobisher struck him as unlikely, he promised to put a word in and quickly changed the subject.

'Another waste of time.' Rafferty muttered as he and Llewellyn climbed back in the car. And given Freddie Talbot's seemingly endless ability to dominate the conversation without saying much of any interest, he had managed to waste plenty of it.

'Fancy' Freddie had struck Rafferty as a vain little man, with his cravat and the walking stick that he used with such emphasis.

When they got back to the station it was to find that forensic had released the pile of birthday cards Clara Mortimer had received on the morning of her death.

There were six of them. Curiously, Rafferty opened them. One was from the Toombses and contained a sentimental little verse about friendship that had presumably been picked by Mrs Toombes rather than her fisherman husband. Their card brought to Rafferty the unwelcome reminder that Mr Toombes had yet to be questioned.

Another of the cards was from Mary Soames and looked to have been hand-painted. After Mrs Soames had gone to such trouble to create a pretty card it was a double shame that Clara Mortimer had never got to see it.

Three of the others seemed to have come from old acquaintances of the sort one didn't see from one year to the next if the hastily scribbled news of the senders' doings during the six months since Christmas were anything to go by. Rafferty was sad to note that the last card in the pile was clearly not from Mrs Mortimer's daughter. The old-fashioned 'real' writing, which the sender shared with Rafferty's ma, made that plain.

The sixth and final card turned out to have come from Freddie Talbot. Rafferty cringed as he read the lover's poem Talbot had penned; it didn't even scan properly, at least to Rafferty's unpractised eye. He handed it to Llewellyn, who smiled and said, 'Mr Talbot's efforts wouldn't have greatly impressed Mrs Mortimer, I fear. Her bookshelves indicate she was an educated lady.'

'Didn't think much of it myself, I must admit,' Rafferty began, before Llewellyn interrupted him.

'If I'm not mistaken, I believe this is part of one of the sonnets Shakespeare was reputed to have written to "the dark lady".' Llewellyn opened his mouth as though to begin to quote.

Rafferty held up his hand. 'Please. Spare me.' He paused and grinned. 'What a sly old goat Freddie Talbot must be. First he sends love poems to Clara Mortimer, then, only today, he professes undying love for Amelia Frobisher and begs me to try to bring her round. It's lucky for him that Miss Frobisher didn't read his little ditty.'

'Maybe she did,' Llewellyn quietly observed. He held up a note that had been returned with the cards. 'According to forensics, this card had been opened and resealed. But whoever did it left their fingerprints on it.'

'Let me guess. They're Miss Frobisher's – right?'

Llewellyn nodded.

All the residents' fingerprints had been taken as a matter of routine, though not without protests, most volubly from Amelia Frobisher, though Rafferty, thankfully, had missed that particular little scene.

'No wonder she's cut Freddie Talbot off without a

home-cooked little dinner to his name,' said Rafferty. 'I suppose Miss Frobisher recognized the writing when she noticed Mrs Mortimer's door was ajar and couldn't resist opening the envelope to see what "Fancy" Freddie had to say to Clara.'

'Probably,' Llewellyn agreed. 'But the important question I would have thought, is whether she saw the card *after* Mrs Mortimer was killed – or before.'

The discovery that Talbot's birthday card to Clara Mortimer had been opened and resealed, together with Llewellyn's weighty question, gave both men much on which to ponder. The other fingerprints – one set of which forensics had already identified as Mrs Mortimer's – presumably belonged to the postal workers handling the mail; certainly none of the other residents' prints had been found on the envelope.

They decided to have an early night and ponder some more before they tackled Amelia Frobisher again.

Rafferty and Llewellyn returned to the station on the Saturday morning to catch up on the mountain of paper-work a murder inquiry inevitably produced. In the back of Rafferty's mind was the question of how best to tackle Amelia Frobisher, but for now, he left the question to soak in his brain, with the hope that his brain would throw up some answers.

Along with the routine stuff was a report from the forensics laboratory that had arrived after they had left the previous evening. The report included a particularly upsetting discovery concerning Clara Mortimer's murder. Not only had someone apparently tried to wipe the victim's living room free of fingerprints, it seemed they had done so whilst dragging the dying woman around the living room with them.

They must have done so, Rafferty concluded. Given that smears of the victim's blood were left at each location where the surfaces had been wiped, what other conclusion was possible?

Upset by this barbarity, Rafferty sat heavily in the chair behind his desk. Surely this latest news put the scrawny Amelia Frobisher out of the running? He couldn't see her having the strength to manhandle Clara Mortimer, who must have been a good stone heavier.

Now he demanded of Llewellyn, 'Mrs Mortimer was an elderly woman. What need was there for her assailant to be so brutal?'

The cooler tempered Llewellyn supplied the logical answer.

'I would presume because such behaviour *was* necessary. Unless her attacker was in some way deranged and found amusement in acts of sadism, I imagine Mrs Mortimer was still conscious at that stage. How else – other than by dragging her around with him – would the murderer have been able to prevent her from hitting one of the panic buttons while he was otherwise occupied in wiping his prints?'

'Why didn't this inept individual just wear gloves?'

Llewellyn shrugged. 'Why didn't Miss Frobisher use a cloth or something similar to hold the envelope of the birthday card when she opened it? People don't think. We both know that many amateur burglars don't bother to go properly equipped. They're opportunists who see an opportunity, take it and realize where they went wrong afterwards.'

'So now you're thinking that Clara Mortimer died because some moron couldn't even manage to make a proper job of burgling a defenceless old lady?'

Llewellyn merely shrugged again and said, 'With this latest discovery, it looks that way, though that conclusion fails to address the question of why Mrs Mortimer let him into her home. It could be that her assailant *was* known to her and left such clues deliberately to confuse matters.'

Did that mean they were back to Amelia Frobisher as a

suspect? Rafferty wondered before he threw the forensic report down on his desk. He gazed at it in disgust, his emotions charged not simply by the brutal treatment Clara Mortimer had received, but also by his continuing dismay that Abra had still not replied to his increasingly desperate appeals for forgiveness.

All his telephone messages remained unanswered, his visits to her flat received no welcome buzz in, only the lonely, no one at home echo.

Where *was* she? More worrying, what was she doing and thinking? With her hormones probably out of kilter she might be capable of anything.

Her silence and the worry this engendered was, to Rafferty, a slow torture. It was only by remaining busy that he could keep the anxiety down to a dull ache. With this thought in mind, after a quick scan of the reports, he decided to leave them till later. After reading about how the elderly Clara Mortimer had been so brutally manhandled he was in the right frame of mind to question Amelia Frobisher about her snooping.

At first, Amelia Frobisher tried to deny tampering with Clara Mortimer's mail. But confronted with the indisputable evidence, she brazened it out.

'I'm sure any woman would have done the same when she saw her chap's handwriting on a card to a rival. I admit I was curious.' Amelia Frobisher's countenance frosted over. 'To think before I read his borrowed poetry I was thinking of taking him back. The nerve of the man, ringing me up, making up to me and asking for my forgiveness when all the time he was still making a play for Clara Mortimer.'

Beside Rafferty, Llewellyn cleared his throat. 'Be that as it may, Miss Frobisher, you must see that your discovery of Mr Talbot's continuing betrayal gives rise to some serious questions; one of them being exactly when you found and opened the card.'

'When I found the card?' What can you mean? You know perfectly well when I found it. Right after I saw Clara Mortimer laid out dead and bloody on the floor.'

In spite of further, rigorous questioning, from this stance Amelia Frobisher wouldn't budge. In fact, instead of budging, she came back at them with an accusation.

'If it hadn't come to this I would have continued to say nothing, but—'

'Say nothing?' Rafferty sat forward, careful this time to evade the sofa's too familiar embrace. 'Say nothing about what exactly?'

'About seeing Freddie Talbot hanging around the apartments on the morning Clara was murdered. I flattered myself he was trying to pluck up the courage to ring *my* bell, but it never rang all that morning. You don't know him. I do and poor Freddie doesn't take rejection well. He never did. I'm surprised he hasn't attempted to murder *me*.'

Miss Frobisher gave what could only be described as a titter as the intonation in her voice more than suggested that Freddie Talbot might well have murdered Clara Mortimer.

Certainly, if what she said about his inability to take rejection was true, the rejection he had received from the late Mrs Mortimer had, from Rita Atkins's account, been withering.

'You can ask Rita Atkins if you don't believe me,' she told them.

'But I understood from Mrs Atkins that she slept late that morning.'

'She may well have done, but if you ask her she'll tell you that Freddie was certainly lurking around the apartments in a most suspicious manner the two previous mornings. We both saw him. In fact we had a little chuckle about the silly man.'

Amelia Frobisher had certainly managed to muddy the waters.

'Come on,' Rafferty said as he propelled himself from the settee and made for the door. 'Let's question Mrs Atkins and see if she can corroborate this.'

Rita Atkins seemed astonished to find herself nodding agreement to Amelia Frobisher's claim.

'But when I asked you if you'd seen anyone hanging about the apartments you told me you hadn't,' Rafferty complained.

'You asked me if I'd seen any *strangers* hanging about,' she was quick to correct him. 'Freddie Talbot's not a stranger. He's been coming round here for months to my knowledge, trotting about after that frosty Frobisher like an obedient poodle. It made me sick to watch him, with his, "Yes, Amelias" and his "No, Amelias". She certainly had him where she wanted him. God knows what either of them got out of the relationship, but I suppose they must both have got what they wanted from the other or why bother?'

Chastened, Rafferty walked out of the apartments, climbed in his car and sat brooding. Now what? he wondered. Every time he turned round he seemed to gather more suspects. Trouble was he wasn't sure how to proceed with any of them.

Llewellyn climbed in the car beside him. 'What now?' he asked.

'God knows,' Rafferty replied. 'I'm damn sure *I* don't.'

'There's always Jane Ogilvie. We haven't yet questioned her about her many lies.'

Rafferty brightened at this reminder. 'You're right. That's a bloody good idea. It's about time she had the opportunity to explain why she lied to us about her father being dead. I feel just in the right mood to sort the wheat of the truth from the plentiful chaff of her lies.'

Eight

B ut, as on the day of her mother's murder, when they got round to Mercer's Lane, Jane Ogilvie wasn't home. Only Darryl Jesmond and her children were there.

It was the first time Rafferty had seen all three half-siblings together. They were as dissimilar as it was possible for siblings – even half-siblings – to be.

Hakim, the half-Arab middle child, could be no more than sixteen, but he already sported a shadowy beard. He had extraordinary honey-coloured eyes that seemed not to need to blink and was, Rafferty thought, far too handsome for his own good.

Aurora, the youngest, was also an attractive child. It was only Charles, the eldest, who seemed to have missed out on the good looks of his half-siblings. Perhaps it was only the warm skin tones of Hakim and Aurora that made Charles look unnaturally pale. Certainly, with his smart suit and reserved manner, he seemed to take after Clara Mortimer far more than did Jane.

Jane's eldest son lived in London. He had told them he had left his last job the previous month and was soon due to start a new position for a financial outfit in the City. Jane had told them he had snatched a few days' break with his family before he joined his new employers and had caught the 6.30 train from London's Liverpool Street Station on the morning of her mother's murder. He had rung his mother on her mobile and arranged to meet her when she finished her night shift and treat her to a café breakfast. He had arrived at the family home with his mother only to find Rafferty and DC Mary Carmody there with the news of his grandmother's murder.

What a homecoming, Rafferty had thought as he had added Charles Ogilvie's name to the growing list of those whose alibis had still to be checked. As if it wasn't bad enough to visit his mother and find Darryl Jesmond in residence, without also learning about the murder of his grandmother.

Mary Carmody had questioned the neighbours again and had learned they were more than willing to gossip about this unwanted band of squatters in their midst. Although the neighbours' teenage daughters had mostly seemed smitten by the broodingly handsome sixteen-year-old Hakim, their mothers all, with only one exception, said that he was a haughty, arrogant youth who acted as if all females were his inferiors. With – in the neighbours' words – a mother who was a slut, and coming from a family that lived in a squat, they had all said much the same: what reason did Hakim think he had for acting so superior?

Hakim Mohammed Abdullah, as the younger boy insisted on styling himself, held himself as proudly as any desert sheik and responded as briefly as possible to their questions. But it was clear, even from his brief responses, that he had resented the white grandmother who had ignored him all of his life. I am a grandson to be *proud* of, his flashing dark honey eyes declared.

And when he spoke of his mother it was apparent that he considered it shameful to have to acknowledge the relationship at all.

'Do not ask me about the woman who gave birth to me,' he told them, with a disdainful lift to his chin. 'It would not be honourable for me to revile her to strangers.'

Darryl Jesmond sniggered at this, which brought an angry flush to Hakim's chiselled olive cheeks.

When questioned as to his whereabouts at the time of his

grandmother's death, he said, 'I was at the local mosque, studying the Doctrine of Islam with the Imam, as my Muslim faith instructs, not murdering the old lady. That is the behaviour of cowardly British youths.' His nostrils flared as he swept a disdainful gaze over the assorted collection of full-blooded Anglo-Saxon and Celtic males currently littering the living room.

Rafferty began to see why Hakim Mohammed wasn't popular with the neighbourhood adults. Bemused that Hakim, who had been born and brought up in Essex, should choose to speak in a stylized manner that indicated English wasn't his native tongue, Rafferty felt a fleeting pity for the youth. Although apparently abandoned by his father and left to Jane's tender maternal mercies, it was clear he believed everything Arabic superior and everything English was to be despised; doubtless he would grow out of it.

Rafferty guessed that if consulted about Hakim's twisted outlook, Llewellyn would tell him that the boy's response revealed the psychological damage brought by his father's rejection. Strange, he thought, how often the undeserving parent received the lion's share of the love. Like mother, like son, for the same was true of Jane – another rejected child who, according to Mary Soames at least, had adored the father who had deserted her.

Hakim, presumably in a desire to emulate his absent Arab father, although aloof and clearly unhappy to be subjected to their questioning, nevertheless managed to retain that exquisite politeness with which Arabs were reputed to treat strangers.

Rafferty could have wished for a bit less politeness and rather more in the way of ready information. The boy refused point-blank to provide the imam's name, doubtless thinking that to speak the man's name in front of infidels would somehow sully his holy virtues.

But, out of a desire to prove that not all 'infidels' were the ill-mannered louts that Hakim clearly believed them to be, Rafferty responded with a similar politeness and didn't press the point. Besides, the last thing he wanted was cultural offence – and all that implied – to rear its head.

To avoid such a clash, he decided it would be prudent to assign to the more culturally sensitive Llewellyn the task of checking Hakim's alibi.

Further questioning of Hakim elicited only an increasingly distant manner along with the implication that, in demanding fuller answers, they were impugning his honour.

At the end of the questions, obviously deeply offended, Hakim retreated to the far end of the room and stared at them in such a brooding manner that Rafferty wondered if the boy was putting some kind of ancient Arabic hex on them.

Frustrated, but only too aware the politically correct thought police that nowadays ruled police actions would – even in a murder inquiry – fail to back him if he continued to demand answers from this determinedly Muslim youth, he turned with relief to the more open-featured Aurora and asked her where she had been at the time of her grandmother's death.

'I was here, getting ready for school.'

'You were alone in the house?'

After a brief hesitation, she nodded.

At least the half-brother's twelve-year-old half-sister was friendlier. A pretty girl with a café-au-lait complexion, Aurora, curled up in the corner of the tatty green settee, looked like a dusky-peach rosebud discarded amongst garden refuse.

Aurora and Darryl Jesmond seemed to have something of a mutual admiration society in operation, Rafferty noted. Because when Jesmond had flung himself down on the settee after answering their rap on the knocker-free door and sat unnecessarily up close and personal to Aurora, she didn't draw back; far from it. With her precocious coquette's hair tossing and eyelash batting, she seemed to be encouraging his attentions.

Little wonder Jane Ogilvie seemed so aggressive and ready to hit out at the world, Rafferty thought, if her own daughter was prepared to compete for Darryl's attentions. He wondered whether the phrase *what price rebellion, now?* didn't occasionally enter Jane's head.

Rafferty was astonished to learn from Jesmond that Jane was at work – though why anything that a member of this family did should still surprise him, Rafferty was unable to fathom.

Jane had already freely revealed her true feelings for her late mother. That she should return to work so soon after Clara Mortimer's brutal murder was par for the course.

Given her sorry lack of grief, Rafferty decided that Jane Ogilvie neither required nor deserved the soft handling a victim's family usually received. If she was so unfeeling as to return to her supermarket shelf-stacking, she must be up to answering some simple questions, particularly as her own lies had provoked the need for them.

He glanced at his watch. It was well after ten. Jane Ogilvie's night shift must surely have finished some time ago. So where was she?

Darryl, when he questioned, merely responded with a noncommittal shrug.

'Where was it you said Mrs Ogilvie worked?' he asked Jesmond.

Darryl managed to tear himself away from Aurora's youthful charms for long enough to drawl, 'I didn't say. But since you ask, it's at the branch of Motson's on Northway, near the swimming pool. They're short-staffed, so I'd guess she's doing a bit of overtime.'

Rafferty nodded, forced out an unwilling 'Thank you.'

Ignored by the sulking Hakim, Rafferty told Charles and the playful pair on the settee that they would see themselves out. Then he and Llewellyn left, to make their way to Jane Ogilvie's place of employment.

But when Rafferty spoke to Mr Empson, the young

manager of the local Motson's supermarket, and asked to speak to Jane Ogilvie, he discovered that Jane had told them more lies. Rob Empson informed them he had sacked her for theft the week before.

It was apparent Jane had chosen not to tell Darryl that she was out of work; Rafferty concluded that Jane must suspect the jobless gigolo Darryl would not be pleased that his milch cow would no longer be able to supply his needs.

This was unsurprising, because Mary Carmody had learned on the neighbourhood grapevine that one of the neighbours – a woman whose divorce had left her financially comfortable – had been making approaches to Darryl, including buying him an expensive watch for his birthday, which Darryl had been more than pleased to accept. How had Jane felt about that? Rafferty wondered.

It struck Rafferty that Darryl Jesmond was hedging his bets. Certainly, until her mother's murder, few of the neighbours had believed that Jane had any hope of keeping the fickle Darryl's affections when she faced such ready-spending competition.

And now? he wondered. If Darryl's gigolo tendencies were anything to go by, Rafferty was with the neighbours in suspecting he would choose to stick with Jane a while longer. There could well be an affluent lifestyle waiting in the wings, if he hung around, was what Rafferty concluded had been Darryl's thoughts.

The reading of Clara Mortimer's will would certainly make for an interesting spectator sport – if it existed at all, which was looking increasingly unlikely as the firm of solicitors Mary Soames had mentioned denied having such a document in their safekeeping.

'So Jane Ogilvie was caught stealing,' Rafferty repeated. 'You didn't prosecute?'

Rob Empson shook his head, squeezed himself past the edge of his desk in his cubbyhole of an office and reached into the filing cabinet.

'Not worth the hassle.' He handed Rafferty a slim buff folder taken from the cabinet. 'That's the brief, unimpressive history of Jane Ogilvie's employment with us. If she hadn't been caught helping herself to our merchandise, she'd have been on the way out anyway. Her timekeeping was worse than most of the part-time teenagers we employ and her treatment of the customers was unfortunate, to say the least. In the modern parlance, she had an *attitude* problem. Jane Ogilvie thought the world – or her mother – owed her a living.'

'You weren't worried she'd take you to a tribunal?' Rafferty asked. But as he glanced through Jane Ogilvie's work record, he realized why Rob Empson's answer was in the negative. It contained plenty of notes about late arrivals and days off sick as well as one written warning.

'Apart from the fact she was still on probation and had already received several verbal and one written warning, she was caught red-handed – literally – trying to leave by the staff exit with half a dozen of our best Scotch fillets in her bag, and a couple of bottles of our most expensive red wine. Stupidly, she hadn't thought to wrap the bottles in something to stop them clinking together. One of our security staff stopped her. They called me and I sacked her on the spot.'

He shrugged. 'It's the firm's policy, instant dismissal – cheaper and more effective than prosecution. Not a lot of point suing someone who has no money and needs to filch stuff from a supermarket to provide her boyfriend with a birthday treat.'

'Has she found another job, do you know?' Rafferty enquired as he handed back the file.

'If she has, she hasn't given my name as a referee. But, in the circumstances, that's scarcely surprising.'

'Was she particularly friendly with any of your staff?'

'She wasn't well-liked. But let me call in a couple of the women she worked nights with most often. They've both transferred to day shifts, so are on duty.' He paused to speak into the store intercom on his desk.

Within a couple of minutes, the already crowded office was verging on rush-hour tube train claustrophobia.

'I'll leave you to it,' Rob Empson volunteered, as, with much breathing-in by all parties, he squeezed past Rafferty, Llewellyn and Jane Ogilvie's shelf-stacking colleagues.

The two work colleagues Rob Empson had selected were both middle-aged women. They claimed Jane was always complaining about lack of money, but as her colleagues testified, this was hardly surprising, as she ran up credit on various department-store cards.

'Up to her ears in debt,' one of her colleagues confided. 'Getting desperate, she was. Of course, that pretty boyfriend of hers cost a packet. You'd think she'd have more sense at her age than to go in for such dainties.'

It was clear that Jane Ogilvie hadn't been well regarded by her female colleagues and, to judge from what they said next, Jane was considered a 'bit of a goer' and no better than she ought to be by her male colleagues.

Could Jane have killed her mother for what she hoped to inherit? Rafferty wondered. And in order to hang on to the faithless Darryl? It seemed evident she kept up the connection with her mother only because she wanted to get money out of her.

After thanking the women, he and Llewellyn went in search of the manager. Rafferty thanked him for his time and told him he could have his office back.

'So where do you reckon Jane spends her nights, seeing as she's no longer stocking her fridge and wine rack from Motson's?' he asked Llewellyn as they wound their way through the supermarket's aisles and out into the pleasant warmth of the bright June morning. 'Keeping tabs on Darryl Jesmond, would be my guess. I'd be keen to know what that young man gets up to through the midnight hours,' he said. 'And if *he* was into anticipating Jane's expected inheritance . . . ?'

As if suspecting that Rafferty was about to start his well-known theorizing in advance of proven facts, as they climbed in the car, Llewellyn said, 'Jesmond struck me as an idle young man. It's clear he lives off women. Can you see him doing something – like murder – which, in this case, required early rising and effort?'

In mitigation, Rafferty countered. 'Maybe – if he saw enough profit in it, which in this case, he would. One morning's early rising, followed by the bashing-in of an old lady's head, could have set him up for life. I think that might appeal to our Darryl. God knows, his claimed alibi isn't up to much.'

Darryl had given the names of a couple of his drinking mates as alibis. He had claimed they had had a late-night gambling session and had crashed out around two in the morning. From what DC Lilley, who had questioned these friends, had said about them, they sounded about as reliable as Jesmond himself.

'Strange then, that Jesmond hasn't put himself out to show Mrs Ogilvie much in the way of love and support. If he expects her to inherit from her mother, I'd have thought he would do his best to keep her favour.'

It was a valid point, certainly. But as Rafferty commented, he thought Darryl belonged to the 'treat 'em mean and keep 'em keen' school of courtship. It was clear, that between Jane, her daughter and the neighbouring divorcée that the method worked for Darryl.

'Let's get back to Mercer's Lane,' Rafferty instructed as Llewellyn slowly made for the exit of the supermarket's car park. 'Maybe Mrs Ogilvie is back home by now.'

As confirmed by Aurora, who opened the door to their knock, Jane Ogilvie had indeed returned home from her 'work' by the time they arrived back at Mercer's Lane.

Of the rest of the family no one was in evidence. The living room to which Aurora led them was empty.

'I suppose you want to ask Mum why she lied to you?'

'You knew she had lied?' Rafferty questioned sharply.

Aurora shrugged. 'I heard her and Dazza arguing about it.' She grinned. 'Few things stay secret in this house, with all the shouting matches that go on. Mum's in her bedroom. I'll call her.'

Aurora went to the door and hollered, 'Mum, the cops are here again. They want to speak to you.'

Aurora turned round and came back into the room while they waited for her mother to join them. 'I don't blame her for lying. Why should my granddad get put in the frame for murdering the old woman?' She paused, then grinned. 'Though our dear grandmamma was right about one thing – my mum *is* a slut. I heard her throwing up this morning; I think she's got another sprog in her belly. She hasn't told Darryl – probably scared he'll do a runner like the rest of the daddies when he finds out.'

Before Rafferty could make any comment on the precociously knowing Aurora's claim, Jane thrust open the living-room door and gazed suspiciously around as if she had felt her ears burning and suspected they had been talking about her.

'Now what?' she demanded, before she threw herself down on the settee like a sulky teenager.

She just gave a defiant shrug when they confronted her with her deceit about her employment.

'What did they expect?' she demanded. 'When you're surrounded by stuff you can't afford to buy on the miserable wages they pay? Naturally, you're going to help yourself. It was one of the perks. Everyone did it.'

'The manager, Mr Empson, didn't seem to think so.'

'What would he know?' Jane demanded scornfully. 'He's a graduate trainee and wet behind the ears. If he'd started as a lowly shelf-stacker he'd have learned the wrinkles that the old hands went in for. I only got caught because I was in a rush and got careless.'

Realizing this line was getting them nowhere, Rafferty questioned her about her other little deceit.

'Why did you tell us your father was dead?'

Jane Ogilvie pulled out a cigarette packet and lighter from her jeans pocket and lit up before she replied; a time-wasting trick with which Rafferty was familiar.

'Why do you think?' she demanded once she had finally persuaded her cheap lighter to work. When she received no answer to this question, she shrugged and added, 'I told you my father was dead because I wanted to save him all the hassle I knew he'd get if you discovered who he was. I knew you'd consider him the chief suspect just because he lived in the same block and was my mother's estranged husband. It's not as if he killed her.'

'You're sure of that? I suppose you must be, considering he's now changed his alibi and says he was with you and your eldest son around the time your mother died.' He paused. 'Is that true, Mrs Ogilvie?'

Although he had reason to doubt she was capable of telling the truth if her life depended on it, he asked anyway, 'So, if all three of you were together around seven on the morning your mother was murdered, as your father now claims, where exactly did this happy family gathering take place? Some all-night café, perhaps?'

As she hesitated, he added, 'Only before you reply, remember we'll check your answer out. You've already told us more lies than enough. Any more and we might begin to suspect *you're* the one with something to hide.'

She stared at him. 'Me? Just because I told a couple of stupid lies, you surely can't think *I* had anything to do with my mother's death?' She gave a bitter laugh. 'I doubt if I'm even in the old bitch's will. Knowing how impossible she was, she's probably left it to a cats' home just to spite me.'

For all Jane Ogilvie's protestations of innocence, Rafferty noted she still hadn't revealed her true whereabouts at the crucial time. He brought this failure to her attention.

She scowled and yelled at him. 'I forget where we were. Just bumming around, I suppose. It was a fine morning, nice for walking. We stopped for some filled rolls and coffee at a working men's caff and sat in that little wooded glade across the footbridge over the river and had breakfast.'

Jane Ogilvie hadn't struck Rafferty as likely to be a keen walker or much of a picnicker either.

'But I understood you met your eldest son and you had breakfast together?'

'That was the original arrangement,' she quickly agreed. 'But then my father rang on my mobile and we decided to have a picnic instead. Check with Charlie, if you like. He'll tell you the same as me and my father. God,' she complained, 'surely I can be forgiven for forgetting such a small detail when I've so much on my mind? First I lose my job, then my mother.' She pulled a face. 'Wonder what I'll lose next?'

Darryl Jesmond, probably, was Rafferty's thought. If she was lucky.

Perhaps Jane had also thought it likely that Darryl Jesmond would be the third loss. If so, the thought didn't please her. Her plain, over-made-up face turned ugly. 'I couldn't even afford to buy my son breakfast. What sort of a crappy life is that? If my mother hadn't been so demanding and controlling I wouldn't have needed to rebel and end my education early, wouldn't now not even be earning the supermarket's poverty wages that left me permanently broke. But she gave me no choice as she thought I didn't have the right to live my life my way.'

Rafferty made no comment, but he thought that considering Jane Ogilvie had gone on to give birth to three children by three different men and miscarried several more, it seemed Clara Mortimer might have been right to fear for her wayward daughter and feel she had very good reasons for trying to control her. Clearly, somebody needed to, if only for the sake of her existing children. And now, if young Aurora was to be believed, Jane was pregnant again.

As he and Llewellyn let themselves out, Rafferty found himself wondering about the child Abra might be carrying. For the first time he thought about it as a potential flesh and blood human being rather than a potential problem who could come between himself and Abra.

He also wondered what it must feel like to be a child created solely – as far as he could see – to punish a parent, as Jane Ogilvie's seemed to have been. Did her children realize what had encouraged their creation? Or had Jane managed to find sufficient maturity to keep such damaging information from them?

He glanced at Llewellyn as they climbed in the car. His sergeant's face was set; his lips formed a thin, tight line as if determined they would form a barrier to speech.

Wisely, for once, Rafferty refrained from commenting. With Llewellyn married to his cousin, Maureen, Rafferty had learned from his ma's sure touch on the female grapevine that Llewellyn and Maureen had decided to try for a family sooner rather than later. He also knew that after over two months of trying, Maureen was still not pregnant.

Of course, it was early days yet, though after encountering the fertile Jane and her brood, it would be surprising if Llewellyn didn't feel a little aggrieved.

Beside him, Llewellyn's sudden torrent of speech revealed his lips had lost the battle with his feelings.

'I never thought I'd hear myself say this about anyone, but that woman, that Jane Ogilvie, or whatever she chooses to call herself, is an aberration.'

Rafferty, as he eased the car out of Mercer's Lane and into the stream of traffic on Eastchepe, mischievously asked, 'Why? Because she had her kids of many colours not because she wanted them for themselves, but simply to get back at her mother?'

'Of course. What sort of reason is that for bringing a child into the world?'

Rafferty hesitated, then decided to plunge straight in. 'In

my experience, some women have kids, not because they want the *kids* themselves, particularly, but because they want to snare themselves a partner. Or because they don't know what else to do with their lives and having kids not only gives them a purpose but more often than not, their own Council flat, too. Others are simply sheep-like and tend to follow the herd and if all their friends and relations are having babies, they decide to have one, too.'

He gave a twisted smile. 'Though, having said that, I don't imagine either of my parents – if they'd been given a glimpse into the future when they got married – would have relished the prospect of producing six little Raffertys.'

And, although, for the sake of his diminishing relationship with Abra, he was trying to come to terms with the idea, in truth, he wasn't relishing the prospect, the possibility, of producing *one* little Rafferty.

'Still,' he added, in an attempt at commiseration, 'when you think of all the people who would make great parents but who can't have kids, it does seem a bit much when women like Jane Ogilvie seem to be able to pop them out with great ease at regular intervals just to spite her mother.'

But even that wasn't strictly true, he silently acknowledged, because between Charles's and Hakim's births, Jane had, according to Mary Soames, suffered several miscarriages.

By now, with Rafferty concentrating on crossing the busy High Street/East Hill junction, preparatory to entering the police station's rear entrance, the ever-cautious Llewellyn fell silent. But his sergeant's brooding thoughts felt so much like a palpable third occupant in the car that Rafferty, once he'd instructed Llewellyn to organize the team into checking out the various alibis they'd been given, was glad to park up and escape to his office.

Nine

Llewellyn made light work of delegating the alibi-checking and when he rejoined Rafferty ten minutes' later, Rafferty was thankful to note that Llewellyn had recovered his equilibrium. He was anxious to review the progress of the investigation and needed the Welshman's logical input.

Rafferty, feet up on the desk and a mug of strong tea at his elbow, was unsurprised that Llewellyn should return with the news that Mary Soames had been correct in her surmise about what had happened to Aurora's long vanished daddy, Earl Ray.

Aurora's father *was* dead, under *all* of his aliases, Llewellyn now revealed. He had been gunned down two years previously in some drug gang war of attrition.

Rafferty nodded, took a gulp of his tea and remarked, 'That leaves young Hakim's father and Jane's ex-husband as the only named outsiders still in the running.'

Though Rafferty had no reason to think either of the men were strong suspects. In the case of Abdullah, it seemed unlikely that the man who had shown no interest in his son's birth or subsequent life, would have returned to England and murdered Jane's mother. But routine checks still had to be gone through. And given the sensitive racial connotations brought by the Arabic background of Hakim's father, Rafferty had judged diplomacy a necessity, so had set Llewellyn the task of tracking him down.

'I think we can now safely cross Jamil Abdullah off the

117

list of suspects,' Llewellyn said. 'I managed to trace him using one of my old university contacts in the Foreign Office. He made a few discreet enquiries. I've just heard back from him. He's discovered that Abdullah *is* back in his native Egypt and, as far as he can ascertain, he hasn't been to England for some years – though, given the shambolic state of the Immigration Service he couldn't give me a one hundred percent confirmation of that.'

'We can't expect miracles,' Rafferty said, before asking, 'Is Mary Carmody back yet? I'm keen to know if she had any joy in learning the present whereabouts of Jane's ex-husband.'

'I saw her come in about five minutes ago. Do you want me to get her to come up?'

'Please.'

Llewellyn picked up the phone and relayed the message.

Mary Carmody came up a few minutes' later and reported what she had found out. She had followed Rafferty's instructions to waylay James Ogilvie's son and question him about his father's current address rather than ask Jane and invite more lies.

She had approached young Charles when he ventured forth from the family squat, she reported.

'I managed to persuade him to let me have his father's current address, though he begged me not to let his mother know they were in regular contact.'

'That doesn't surprise me,' Rafferty commented. 'It must be hell being the kid of divorced parents, especially when one of them is Jane Ogilvie. She's never struck me as the kind of woman to be reasonable when it came to her ex having parental contact.'

From his seat in the corner, Llewellyn butted in. 'She didn't, to me, seem the type of woman who would be reasonable about *anything*, never mind something as emotive as parental rights.'

'So, where is James Ogilvie living now?' Rafferty asked Mary Carmody.

'He's moved abroad. France. He's married again and has several more children.'

What a talent Jane had for driving her exes either out of this world, as with Aurora's dad, or out of the country, as with her ex-husband and young Hakim's father, thought Rafferty.

Mary Carmody told him she had just come off the phone after speaking to James Ogilvie. He claimed to have been in a business meeting in the Australia branch of his firm at the time Clara Mortimer died. He had even supplied half a dozen names to verify his claim.

'I've started the ball rolling with our Australian opposite numbers to get confirmation of Ogilvie's claim,' Mary said.

'That's fine. Thanks, Mary.'

After he had dismissed Carmody, Rafferty said to Llewellyn, 'Given Ogilvie's remarriage, the fact that he is able to contact his son whenever he likes and the number of witnesses he's produced to back up his story, Ogilvie seems destined to join Jamil Abdullah on the out-of-the-running list. Which – apart from the other residents still under suspicion and "Fancy" Freddy Talbot – leaves us with Jane Ogilvie, her assorted brood and her recently disinterred "dead" father. Certainly, Harry Mortimer and Jane must both be prime suspects. At least until we find the will that leaves her money to the cats' home that Jane claimed probable.' Though the finding of such a document was looking increasingly unlikely.

Rafferty told Llewellyn that he suspected the pair of collusion, given that they now claimed they had been together at the time of Clara's death. 'And maybe they *were* together,' he added, 'in Clara's apartment, killing the old lady for the inheritance, using Jane's son as an unlooked-for but undoubtedly welcome alibi bonus.'

'It's a possibility, of course.' Llewellyn sounded doubtful about this. 'But if we look at Jane Ogilvie's previous relationships, they indicate she's nothing more than a weak, immature woman whom men used and discarded. From her abandonment by her father, to her marriage to Ogilvie – which bears all the hallmarks of an unwilling shotgun marriage – to her relationships with the fathers of her two younger children, each succeeding relationship put her on a downward spiral. It seems to me that Jane Ogilvie, used to having a *controlling* mother, simply got herself into a succession of 'controlling' relationships with men. Of which her latest, with the much younger Darryl Jesmond, who seems to me to have her exactly where he wants her, is, in many ways, the saddest of them all.

'And then there's her aggressive attitude towards her mother, even now she's dead – especially now she's dead – which makes me the more inclined to think she had nothing to do with Clara Mortimer's murder. I can't see the immature Jane – who produced her mixed-race babies to upset her mother – likely to have sufficient sense to produce aggression as a form of alibi, one that says, *If I had killed my mother, would I be so foolish as to let you know my real feelings towards her?*'

'Oh, I think Jane Ogilvie has sense enough to realize that even though Clara Mortimer seems to have done her best to keep them at arm's length, some of the apartments' other elderly residents may well have figured out Jane's true relationship with her mother, especially given the argument Darryl had with Mrs Mortimer. The apartment's residents are all retired, all with time on their hands and mostly single females at that, with the usual female inquisitiveness. Knowing she could scarcely deny it, Jane, it seems to me, may well have concluded it was better to make a defiant virtue of her poor relationship with her mother.'

Rafferty drained the rest of his tea and added, 'I think we should concentrate more on just how far Jane Ogilvie would go to keep that wandering-eyed toy boy, Darryl Jesmond, who until her mother's death seemed to be sending out feelers – and more than feelers – to find a cosy billet with one of the neighbours.

'We've already discovered her capacity for deceit. Not only did she tell us her father was dead, she also concealed the fact that she had been sacked for theft, which concealment must have been prompted by the worry that jobless and moneyless, she would be unable to hang on to Darryl.

'And then there's Darryl Jesmond himself; an unpleasant young man who lives off women. How tempting would *he* have found it to rid the world of Jane's mother so he could get his hands on what Jane must have told him she would inherit?

'Did you notice how up close and personal Darryl Jesmond seems to be with Jane's young daughter, Aurora?' Rafferty now asked.

Llewellyn nodded.

Certainly that young lady, in the short time Rafferty had known her, seemed to do all she could to encourage Jesmond's attentions. What must Jane feel about that? Would it make her even more desperate? Or more ready to move on to an even more destructive relationship?

'Jane Ogilvie's nearly forty. Given what she said to me and Mary Carmody about the "Plain Jane" tag, middle age must have made her more desperate. She couldn't know for sure where her mother had left her money. But she must have realized, from what Mary Soames said, that the odds were in her favour that her mother *hadn't* made a will; all the more reason, then, to take her chances on inheriting a wad of cash under the intestacy rules.'

As he explained to Llewellyn, although, on the surface, at least, Jane Ogilvie seemed an aggressive person, he thought Mary Soames, in describing Jane as *needy*, had accurately described Jane's personality.

'Even if she had nothing to do with her mother's murder, don't you think that the "needy" Jane, who adored her father, and who openly admitted she resented, even hated, her mother – would be more than ready to provide her father with an after-the-fact alibi and persuade her immature eldest son to back them up?'

Although Llewellyn still appeared unconvinced by his arguments, Rafferty nodded to himself. He could easily see the needy little girl in Jane's psyche being prepared to do whatever it took to regain the love of the adored father who had abandoned her as a child.

Rafferty, who, from Llewellyn, had absorbed a certain amount of pseudo-psychology, thought Jane's aggression concealed a damaged soul, a vulnerable little girl who had never been quite good enough for her parents' love. What more natural than that Jane, the Plain Jane who felt unloved and used rebellion, even in to adulthood, as a form of defence, should use aggression against her mother as her best self-defence?

When he had mentioned some of his thoughts on these lines to his sister, Maggie, her only comment had been, 'Oh, Jar. Can you not see that this Jane is simply a woman who's not good at being on her own? She'd rather have a man – any man – than face up to being alone.'

'I can see that. I understand that,' Rafferty had retorted. And he could see it, more or less – hadn't he got in to such difficulties during his last case because he'd been feeling alone and lonely? Not that even his favourite sister knew about the problems he had experienced back in April. But the difference between himself and Jane Ogilvie was that bitter experience had taught him that loneliness was preferable to being in a lonely partnership with the wrong person.

He had gained this knowledge painfully, during his marriage to Angie, his late wife. That marriage had brought home to him that that sort of loneliness was worse, far worse, than being 'alone'.

Jane's biggest problem, he thought, was that her father hadn't been around when she had been a young girl. Harry Mortimer struck Rafferty as having always been too concerned with his own needs to have enough love or concern to spare for his 'needy' and plain little daughter.

Llewellyn it was, Rafferty thought, who had once said to him that young girls learned how to give and receive love from their fathers. And if their fathers didn't show them affection or were absent in some way, little girls were not only less likely to be able to form loving, male/female relationships, they often spent the rest of their lives searching for the love they had never had, often in damaging partnerships. Jane Ogilvie's relationship record demonstrated the truth of this.

And after such a damaged childhood, what, for Jane, could be more damaging than to have her selfish, irresponsible father re-enter her life and ask her to prove her love for him by protecting him from the latest consequences of his actions?

Although naturally inclined to think most modern psychobabble so much hogwash, Rafferty conceded that there might be something in that particular claim about little girls and their fathers.

On the other hand, he argued to himself while the conscientious Llewellyn went through the latest reports, surely the same thing applied to sons and their mothers?

He had known since he was a toddler that he was his ma's blue-eyed boy, yet here he was, rapidly heading towards 40 and it was only now that he was thinking about settling down with a woman he truly loved – if, that was, given their current difficulties, when she finally surfaced, Abra decided to have him at all.

His mind returned to his and Llewellyn's conversation about Jane Ogilvie and her aggression towards her mother. Llewellyn had made clear that he considered such an open aggression made Jane the less likely to be her mother's murderer.

But – and it was an important but – Llewellyn's reasoning about the likelihood of Jane killing her mother only applied if they were considering Jane without her father.

Rafferty suspected that the sums would come out rather differently if, as their latest alibi indicated, Harry Mortimer entered the equation.

Jane Ogilvie – like Rafferty, heading for her 40s, with a figure not improved by childbearing – struck him as a typical product of her generation; so many of whom never seemed to have really grown up. They were the 'me' generation, encapsulated in the lifestyle of the eternal teenager; with the too-short skirts, the unsuitable boyfriends and sexual habits which might be OK for a year or two while one 'found oneself', but which were not a good idea to continue at length, certainly not for the length of time that Jane had carried them on.

Maybe now, with no mother to rebel against, Jane Ogilvie would finally begin to grow up; unless, of course, she *was* guilty of the murder of her mother, either alone or in collusion with her father, in order to bring about the release of the funds which Jane certainly, and her father possibly, seemed to need so desperately. If she *had* murdered her mother, Rafferty could foresee little hope of a happy maturity for Jane.

Ten

By now, Rafferty's head was so full of thoughts he felt past getting a grip on any of them.

He checked with Llewellyn as to whether the latest reports carried anything of interest and when Llewellyn replied in the negative, he said, 'I don't know about you, Dafyd, but I reckon we both deserve an early night. Too much work makes a man *and* his brain dull and I can't help feeling we're missing something important. Maybe a good night's sleep will yet supply us with our "eureka" moment in this investigation.'

After a surprisingly restful night, given the several anxieties currently besetting him, Rafferty arrived bright and early at the station on Sunday morning. He was so early that he even beat Llewellyn in, which was a pity, he thought as he observed the latest reports piled on his desk awaiting his attention. Llewellyn was the paperwork wallah. Rafferty much preferred his sergeant to give him a brief resumé of their contents.

After arming himself with strong tea from the canteen, Rafferty made a start on the pile. He was skim-reading his way through when Llewellyn arrived.

Distracted, Rafferty gave a brief nod in response to Llewellyn's greeting. After skimming through the current report, he put it face down to the left of the pile and picked up the next.

As his gaze flew over the typed report, Rafferty's heart

started hammering as he realized they might just have found their first breakthrough.

After he had read the report through a second time, he gave a wide grin and handed it over to Llewellyn.

'Take a look at that,' he invited. 'I think we might just have found our "eureka" moment.'

This latest report was on the alibi provided by yet another member of the murdered woman's family the checking of which he had set Llewellyn to organize the previous day.

It revealed yet another disturbing discrepancy.

'What a family they are for telling lies,' Rafferty remarked as he and Llewellyn climbed in the car. 'Wonder how many more they'll feel it necessary to concoct before this case is concluded?'

Charles Ogilvie, the latest member of the family whom they had caught out in a falsehood, was still in bed when they called round at the family home. Rafferty despatched his half-sister, Aurora, from her seat on the settee next to Darryl Jesmond to rouse him.

When he finally appeared some twenty minutes later, Charles looked haggard and bleary eyed, with the trembling hands that brought back for Rafferty unwelcome reminders of his own mornings-after sufferings following too many bibulous nights.

Given his increasingly haggard looks, this morning it was extraordinarily easy, in Charles, to see his grandfather as a young man. But although Charles's haggard countenance and bleary eyes betokened a heavy night, Jane's eldest had made some effort to make himself presentable, though Rafferty soon discovered that the young man's ablutions hadn't included the provision of an essential wash and brush-up to his previous answers.

'Mr Ogilvie?' Rafferty again addressed his question to the bent head of Charles Ogilvie as he slumped in the thread-bare green armchair. 'I asked you where you were on the morning your grandmother died. You may have met your mother and grandfather for a picnic breakfast as you and they claim, but what you *didn't* do was travel up from Liverpool Street on the early train. It was cancelled. So when *did* you arrive?'

Charles eventually admitted, 'I arrived the day before.'

'So why lie about it?' Rafferty asked.

Charles Ogilvie blinked and protested. 'But I didn't lie.' He frowned. 'At least, I don't *think* I did.'

Roused suddenly from his sleep as he had been, Charles exhibited an uncertainty that seemed to agitate him. He stuttered and stammered and seemed unable to put together a coherent sentence.

His sister, Aurora, although considerably younger, was clearly made of more steely stock. Suddenly, she came to Charles's defence and rounded on Rafferty.

'Why don't you leave Charlie alone?' she demanded. 'He couldn't have had anything to do with our gran's death. He didn't even know where she lived. Mum never stopped going on about the fact that she hadn't heard from him for months. Charlie hasn't been in touch since the old woman moved into that sheltered block at the new year.

'Besides, he was her pet, the only one of her grandkids she bothered to send birthday and Christmas presents to. The miserable old cow never sent me or Hakim anything, ever.'

As though sensing they would infer resentment on her part for this failure, she added, 'That wasn't his fault. Me and Hakim knew that. We've never held it against him.'

Charles looked so startled by this claim that Aurora's pretty face flushed and she added, 'Well, not much. And even if we had, he's still our brother – half-brother. He's *family*, so don't you come round here with your suspicions and your leading questions, 'cos I won't let him answer them, him or Hakim.'

Rafferty, with the impression that Charles felt guilty about being the only one of the three with both a legitimate father and a grandmother who sent him presents, was secretly amused and rather admiring of the young Aurora's staunch championship of her elder brother.

He wondered if she would put up quite such a sterling defence on behalf of her mother if he were to reveal that he now remembered it *hadn't* been Charles who had lied about the precise date of his arrival – that had been Jane.

Had she unwisely lied to them in the rash, unthinking belief that in doing so she would strengthen both her own and her father's alibis? If so, her lie had caught her out.

Although Charles, at least, hadn't contradicted her claim – bitter experience had probably taught him not to contradict his mother when she bent the truth for her own advantage – now Rafferty recalled that Darryl Jesmond *had* looked surprised at her claim. Certainly, Rafferty recalled Jesmond had begun to say something when he had thought better of it.

It was unfortunate for Jane that the train she claimed her son had been on had been cancelled, thus exposing her as a liar for the third time. She had even brazenly challenged them to check her son's alibi, he recalled. She must have more confidence in the country's transport system than most of its *customers*, he thought. Or perhaps it was more a case, as Llewellyn had commented, that her temperament was of the type that acted first and thought afterwards.

Now, as Charles Ogilvie revealed he had actually arrived the previous day, rather than on the morning of his grandmother's murder, Rafferty wondered why the young man had been carrying a suitcase – and what it contained – when he and Jane had finally turned up after his and Mary Carmody's arrival to break the news of the murder.

To judge from his anxious countenance, Charles Ogilvie seemed concerned that he might inadvertently spill several sorts of beans. He had begun to stammer an attempt at an answer but this attempt soon reverted to a silence that was even more intriguing especially when it came not only in the face of Rafferty's continuing questions, but also when, shamefully for Charles, his defence seemed reliant on his little sister fighting his corner for him. What could he be concealing when the latter humiliation was insufficient to stir him to speech?

Even the younger Hakim bridled at his younger sister's attempt to speak for him.

'If I choose to answer questions or not answer them, I shall do so,' Hakim now told Aurora haughtily. 'I do not need a little girl to speak up for me. If your brother has insufficient pride in his manhood and honour that he lets—'

'*Our* brother,' Aurora was quick to correct Hakim.

Hakim ignored the interruption. 'If *your* brother is so lacking in manhood that instead of speaking for himself he lets you do it for him he has no business calling himself a man. Whereas I—'

Whatever Hakim had been about to proclaim got no further, as just then, Jane Ogilvie, dressed in a skimpy black dressing gown that revealed legs decorated with thread veins, entered the room.

In a tight repressed voice that was unlike her usual speaking voice, she told her younger son, 'All right, Kimmy, put a sock in it.'

To Rafferty's surprise, this morning, instead of exhibiting 'need' or aggression, Jane seemed to have discovered a new resolve. Was it the desire to protect her father that had brought it about? he wondered.

It seemed that even Hakim recognized the new authority in his mother's voice, for although he bridled at the childish 'Kimmy' diminutive, after casting one burning glance at Jane, both his boasts about his own manhood and his taunts to Charles about his lack of same came to an abrupt, if simmering halt.

'And yes, Inspector,' Jane turned her attack on Rafferty,

'as he has just told you, Charles *did* arrive the day before my mother's death. But it was *me* who told you that, not my son, so take it out on me, not him. And as for the question I sense hovering on your lips, the suitcase Charles carried contained our family laundry. I picked it up before I met Charles for breakfast and he was sweet enough to insist on carrying it for his mother, especially as I told him I'm preg—'

Jane broke off, her oh-so-recent air of authority vanished. She cast an anxious glance at Darryl, who was lounging in the corner smirking as the latest in-house entertainment rolled by.

Jane hadn't broken off quickly enough as became evident when Darryl's smirk vanished. His tanned face darkened several shades as he leapt up from his seat and covered the floor space between himself and Jane in two strides.

He thrust his face inches from Jane's and demanded aggressively, 'Especially as you're what?'

Jane backed away. Involuntarily her hand went to her belly in a protective gesture.

The gesture didn't escape Darryl. He moved forward, his hand raised as if to strike her and Jane took another hurried step back.

Darryl stared at her, his face full of loathing. 'I get it. You bloody bitch. Did you really think you could saddle me with one of your bastards?' he shouted at her.

Before the situation had a chance to turn even nastier, Rafferty intervened.

'All right. All right. Let's calm things down here.' To Jesmond, he unthinkingly remarked, 'Surely the responsibility for any child is as much *yours* as Mrs Ogilvie's?'

His intervention rebounded on him – because, as his zealous Catholic conscience wasn't slow to remind him – couldn't the same be said to apply to himself and the baby Abra suspected she was carrying? Was he as bad as the feckless Jesmond, after all?

Well, perhaps he wasn't quite as bad, he consoled himself as his remark was greeted with scorn by Darryl.

'Just as much *my* responsibility?' Jane's toy boy jeered.

'Hardly. With *her* track record? Who could blame me for believing she must, by now, have learned something about contraception?'

Darryl gave the cowering Jane a dirty look, then barged past Llewellyn and slammed out of the house.

After a few seconds' awkward silence, Jane spoke in a determined, if shaky voice, to upbraid her daughter.

'I heard you shouting as I came along the hall. If you have nothing better to do than have a go at the policemen investigating my mother's murder, you can get yourself down to the corner shop. We've nothing in for this evening's meal.'

'Don't tell me what to do,' Aurora immediately stormed at Jane. 'I won't be *told* what I'm to do and not do. Jeez, man, you're getting just like that dead old mother of yours that you always used to complain about.'

Jane reared back at this. 'What do you mean?' she demanded. 'I'm nothing like my mother.'

'Yeah. Right.' Aurora laughed this claim to scorn and shot a look of triumph at Jane. Clearly relishing the discovery that she had found a stick with which to beat her mother, she set about using it with a will.

'So you're not bossy and blinkered and convinced your way's the only way to do anything, just like you always told us she was?' Aurora demanded before she shook her head. 'I've seen the photos of her that Charlie used to keep in his room when he was younger. Funny, but the older you get, the more like her you become.' Cruelly, she added, 'Next, you'll be seeing her face when you look in the mirror. Isn't that what they say happens? Middle-aged women turn into their mothers?' She touched her mixed race, café-au-lait skin. 'I'm safe from that, at least.'

Jane didn't react for a few seconds, but when she did, it

was with a ferocity that was totally unexpected, not least by Aurora.

Jane slapped her daughter's face so hard that the girl's head jerked violently on her neck.

'Don't you dare taunt me with my mother,' she screamed at the girl. 'She's dead, or have you forgotten?'

Aurora's eyes filled with tears. But they were tears that Rafferty guessed Aurora was determined not to shed. As if she would force them back, with an unnecessary harshness she rubbed the cheek where her mother had struck her and where the finger marks were visible. As she blinked back her tears, she stared at her mother with a wordless fury.

But Aurora's silence didn't last long. Rallying, she quickly found words designed to wound and screamed back, 'Don't pretend you cared a toss for your mother. We all know you hated her. God knows, you made it plain often enough. The only thing you loved about her was her money that you used to buy Darryl's attention.'

The precocious Aurora, with the ruthless confidence of youth and beauty, delivered the coup de grâce to her middle-aged mother. 'At least I never needed to resort to bribes to get him to pay me attention. If you knew how many times he's tried to get in to my knickers . . .'

When Jane, obviously stunned, failed to respond, Aurora added dismissively, 'As if I'd want him. I only played up to him to get to you. But I think we both know where Dazza will be headed if your old mother has left her money to some cats' home. He'd trample over us all in his rush to move in with Mrs Rich Divorcée down the road.'

White-faced, Jane stared at her daughter. In spite of her previous throwaway remark that her mother had probably left her out of her will, it was clear that Jane hadn't really believed the conventional Clara would actually *do* so. But Aurora's sharp retort had clearly brought the possibility home to Jane. Not only that, but Aurora's prediction about Darryl Jesmond's likely reaction if Aurora's taunt turned out to be true seemed likely to make her mother lash out once more.

But after a quick glance at Rafferty as if just recalling his presence, Jane got herself under control and instead of slapping her daughter again, she just hissed, 'Get out of my sight. And if I catch you making your harlot's eyes at Darryl again, you'll get another slap.'

With a 'see if I care' shrug, Aurora made the second slammed-door exit of the morning, leaving a strained silence behind her.

Happy families, Rafferty mused. What was it that Llewellyn quoted about them? Something some Russian bloke had said, he thought, though his musings on this didn't get the chance to get beyond first base, as after raking a hand through her untidy hair, Jane gave a shaky laugh as if to prove she was unmoved by her daughter's remarks.

'Kids,' she said, as she raised her eyes to heaven. 'Who'd have 'em?'

Although she tried to shrug off Aurora's comments, she was clearly rattled by them. But she rallied sufficiently to have another go at Rafferty, as if still convinced that aggression was her best defence.

'You seem to have a down on my eldest son,' she accused, adding tartly, 'and as he seems unable to speak up for himself, if you've got anything else to ask him you'd better do so while I'm here to do it for him.'

For a moment, Rafferty was surprised that Jane should belatedly exhibit a previously unsuspected maternal streak in thus defending the defenceless Charles. But, of course, her latest attempt at the old 'best defence is aggression' ploy wasn't necessarily put on for her son's sake. Clearly, Charles didn't share the family fluency for lies. Jane couldn't risk him blurting out anything else; next time he might just incriminate either her adored father or herself.

Rafferty was just considering inviting Charles to accompany them to the station so they could get at the truth without

Jane's intervention – he was legally of age, after all. But Charles's bemused looks persuaded him that such a step might not be necessary after all. Instead, he decided to reply to Jane's challenge.

'Now you mention it, yes, there *was* one other thing I wanted to ask him.'

He turned back to Charles. 'We've contacted your previous employers and it seems you weren't head-hunted at all. Not only do you not have a new employer, your previous employers sacked you for unreliability.' Another family trait? Rafferty mused. 'Perhaps it will be second time lucky,' Rafferty added slyly as, again, Charles failed to come up with an answer, 'seeing as you failed to explain why you went along with your mother's lies about the day of your arrival. I'm waiting,' he told Charles. 'I'm curious to see if you can manage to come up with some answers, all on your own this time, to explain the latest Ogilvie family deceit in this investigation.'

Charles, for all his fancy suits, looked like a little boy again – a little boy about to cry. His nose began to run. He wiped it quickly with the back of his hand. He looked to his mother; he didn't look in vain. Whatever claim Hakim might make about his elder brother's lack in the manhood department, he certainly wasn't short on stalwart feminine defenders as Jane rounded on Rafferty for the third time.

'So he was sacked? So what? It's hardly a hanging offence. The best of us have been sacked at one time or another.'

'I'm not disputing that,' Rafferty told her. As he had come pretty close to being sacked – and worse – once or twice himself, he admitted he wasn't in a position to argue with her assertion. 'But the fact is your son deliberately deceived us.'

For that matter, so had Jane, who had claimed she had still been on duty at the supermarket around the time her mother died. Now, here was another member of Clara Mortimer's family without an alibi – or rather, between

Jane, her father and now her son – with an insubstantial triangle of self-supporting alibis which looked to have no more strength than thistledown.

'I don't know why you're picking on Charlie,' Jane said to Rafferty. 'Why on earth should you think *he* would want to hurt the grandmother that loved him? That opinionated daughter of mine is right about one thing. Charlie *didn't* know my mother's address. He hasn't been in touch since before she moved, so how *could* he know it?'

Her obvious disgruntlement at this lack of filial devotion caused Charles's head to droop even further and a 'Sorry, Mum. I did mean to get in touch,' rose up from his downcast head.

'Yes, well. Try a bit harder in future.'

Jane turned her attention back to Rafferty. 'It would make more sense if you picked on one of my other kids, as they had no reason to love my mother, but Charlie?'

'Then if he's got nothing to hide he won't mind telling me where he really was around seven o'clock that morning.' When Charles's head still hung, Rafferty said, 'I'm waiting, Mr Ogilvie.'

'I—'

But before Charles could utter more than that one, strangled word, Jane interrupted. 'If you must know, he was waiting outside the supermarket for me to finish work. Darryl hadn't exactly made him feel welcome when he arrived the previous day, so he decided to clear out of the house early before Darryl got up and stay out till Darryl went for his regular visits to the bookies and the pub around eleven. Happy now?'

'So why couldn't you tell me that before?' Rafferty asked Charles.

Charles shrugged. 'I don't know. I suppose I was still feeling raw about getting fired. I was worried about how I'd pay my rent. And I've got some debts . . .' He tailed off and added lamely, 'I suppose I wasn't thinking straight.'

He'd managed, unprompted by his mother, to think straight enough to lie about his employment, was Rafferty's first thought. 'So you hadn't told your son you'd lost your job at the supermarket?' he asked Jane.

Jane shook her head. 'I didn't want to worry him. He knows how tight money's been around here lately. Besides, I didn't want Darryl to know. I thought if my kids knew I was out of work again one of them might have blurted it out to Darryl.'

The words *particularly that little madam, Aurora* hung unspoken in the air.

'So what did you do when your mother didn't appear at the supermarket's staff exit after her presumed night shift?' Rafferty asked Charles.

'I asked a couple of the other women where she was.' He pulled a face. 'They told me she'd been sacked. So I gave her a ring on her mobile and she came and got me.'

'And what time was it when she collected you?'

'About six thirty.'

'I'd have been on time to meet him, too, if the drying machine at the Laundromat hadn't been playing up,' Jane complained. 'And he'd have been none the wiser about my getting the sack.'

Rafferty gave a sigh. Jane Ogilvie had more stories than the Bible. Determined to pin her down as to the accuracy of *one* of her, her son's and her father's so-called alibis, he questioned her further. 'I presume you reported the faulty machine to the Laundromat manager?'

Jane shook her head. 'I couldn't. He wasn't there. He'd left a note on the door saying he'd been called away to another one of the shops.'

'What about other customers?'

'There weren't any. I was the only one there.'

Convenient for Jane, if not for Rafferty, Llewellyn and the investigation. In the unlikely event that she was telling the truth this time, the note she claimed the manager had left on the door might back up her story. Rafferty got her to supply the Laundromat's location so he could have the manager questioned, then he and Llewellyn left, it becoming clear to Rafferty that they would get nothing further from either Jane or Charles.

Even Hakim, who had earlier spoken contemptuously about Charles's manhood, stared defiantly at Rafferty and offered no further comment.

The Ogilvie family were closing ranks. They might all be at loggerheads, their expressions said, but they would stand together against any police inclination – as they would no doubt regard it – to turn one of them into a scapegoat.

Of course, as Rafferty remarked to Llewellyn on their way out, these defensive family walls held a weak link in the form of Darryl Jesmond.

And like all weak links, Rafferty thought Jesmond would repay a little probing. Now he had discovered Jane was expecting a fourth 'happy event' Jesmond might be less prepared to plaster over the cracks of the family's many lies than he had been before.

Eleven

They found Darryl Jesmond in the nearest pub. He was in a side booth, chatting up a woman whom Rafferty assumed from her costly, but unsubtle jewellery and expensive-looking, low-cut top that exposed a more than generous expanse of creamy bosom, must be the *Mrs Rich Divorcée* that Aurora had mentioned.

The chatting up was obviously going well as a matchstick wouldn't have fitted between the pair so closing entwined were they.

The lady into whose ear gigolo Jesmond was whispering sweet nothings exuded money in anyone's language. And although even the skilfully applied make-up couldn't conceal the fact that she must have been several years older than Jane Ogilvie, to Jesmond she must have appeared an increasingly more attractive proposition than a Jane whose financial future was not only uncertain, but mired in murky murder.

The shining sweep of chestnut curls brushing against Darryl's shoulder had received a far more professional colouring job than poor Jane's home-bleached blonde locks. From the immaculate make-up and the purse as well stuffed as a chipmunk's cheeks, peeping as tantalizingly from the top of her open handbag as her bosom from her blouse, to her encouraging strokes of Darryl's tanned and well-muscled arm, she clearly had the wherewithal to catch a baker's dozen of the world's Darryl Jesmonds.

Off with the old and on with the even older, was Rafferty's cynical thought as he assessed the cooing lovebirds.

So absorbed were they in each other that Rafferty had to tap Jesmond on the shoulder to attract his attention.

Jesmond's expression became thunderous when he turned and saw who had done the tapping.

'This is harassment,' he complained. 'I've a good mind to make an official complaint.'

'That's up to you, sir,' Rafferty blandly remarked. 'But as you rushed out of the house before I could speak to you further, I thought I'd take my chances at your local. We've one or two questions we believe you may be able to help us with.'

'Who are these gentlemen, Darryl?' Mrs Rich Divorcée murmured in a suitably husky voice as her warm, dark eyes swept a bold, assessing glance over them.

Rafferty could feel the waves of embarrassment emanating from Llewellyn at this frank scrutiny; even marriage, it seemed, couldn't save the Welshman from his unfortunate predilection to blushing when scrutinized by the more forward members of the fairer sex.

'Coppers,' Darryl muttered. 'They're looking into the death of Jane's mother. Can you give us a few minutes, hon?'

Mrs Rich Divorceé, if such she was, pouted becomingly at this dismissal.

'I'll let you boys have your little chat,' she said to Darryl. 'But,' she warned, in a voice from which some of the previous warmth had vanished, 'make sure it *is* no more than a few minutes, *hon*, or I might be forced to find myself other male company.'

After she had slid her swaying, voluptuous femininity past Darryl and Rafferty, she lingered a while in front of the blushing Llewellyn, then, with a low-throated laugh, she sashayed over to the bar, where, much to Darryl Jesmond's obvious chagrin, she quickly attracted the thrusting attentions of a bevy of lunching business types.

After he had directed a warning frown in the direction

of the competition, Jesmond turned back, scowled at Rafferty and issued the churlish invitation, 'Well, get on with it, then. I haven't got all day.'

'And there was me envying you your leisure hours,' Rafferty retorted in the soft voice that Llewellyn was always advising him turned away wrath. 'I didn't realize being a bone-idle gigolo was such a taxing profession. Still –' he glanced towards the bar and then down at Jesmond's wrist, on which the birthday present watch bought for him by the lady at the bar gleamed with gold's unique sheen – 'the perks look good.'

Before Jesmond could offer a response to this, Rafferty and Llewellyn sat down in the booth, up close and uncomfortably personal – from Jesmond's viewpoint – one either side of Jesmond.

Their close proximity seemed to worry Darryl. To conceal his betraying body language, Jesmond leaned back as if at ease – no doubt for the benefit of his lady friend at the bar, who eyed them with amusement before she tapped her watch to indicate that the precious minutes she had so graciously granted for their talk were passing.

'Perhaps you can explain something to me, Mr Jesmond,' Rafferty began. 'I wondered what prompted Mrs Ogilvie to lie about her son's day of arrival. You failed to contradict her when she told us her son had left London the morning of her mother's murder. Why was that exactly?'

'I *did* contradict her,' Jesmond blustered, before, with a frown, he must have recollected the true version of events as outlined by Rafferty. 'At least I started to. Then I thought, What the hell?'

Jesmond put on an unconvincing display of loving solicitude for his middle-aged partner. 'I thought Jane had enough grief, with police in her living room, without me calling her a liar in front of you.'

'Very chivalrous of you, I'm sure.'

Darryl gave a Tony Blair 'I'm that kind of guy' shrug and took a giant gulp of his lager.

Just then, a harassed young mother with a screaming baby in her arms entered the bar and headed for the beer garden. Their arrival must have reminded Darryl of his own prospective fatherhood, for he gave a ferocious scowl. His next remark revealed a noticeable lack of chivalry.

'Besides, I knew how she felt about her mother. I couldn't help but wonder afterwards if Jane *hadn't* had something to do with the old woman's death and was using the lie about Charlie as a shield; I wouldn't put it past her. She can be a devious bitch. I mean – look at how secretive she's been about this latest brat she's breeding.'

Darryl folded his arms decisively across his manly chest and for the first time met Rafferty's eye readily. 'It's *her* you should be questioning, not me. Though God knows, you're not likely to get much sense out of that daft mare, seeing how oddly she's been behaving lately.'

'Oddly?' Rafferty questioned. 'In what way?'

Darryl shrugged. 'I wondered if she was starting an early change of life. After all –' the much younger Darryl gave a man-to-man snigger – 'she *is* nearly forty. They do say that some women's brains go haywire when they get to the change.'

Jesmond must have recalled that Jane was certainly *not* having an early menopause, for he scowled again. 'Know better now, though, don't I? Bloody bitch. If she thinks—'

'Never mind that for now,' Rafferty interrupted what was obviously going to be another rant at Jane and the fates for his unwanted fatherhood. 'Let's get back to what you said before about Jane behaving oddly. Could you be a bit more specific?'

'Well, let me see. There are a couple of things I can think of right off the top of my head. Take that argument with her mother, for instance. Jane started it. There was I painting the old bag's living room, good as gold, the old woman stirring the paint and bringing me tea and biscuits. Then Jane turns up and starts having a go at her mum.

'Me and old Mrs Mortimer had been getting along fine before that, much better than I'd expected after hearing Jane go on about her mother. But once Jane turned up, before I knew it, she had managed to turn the old girl's question as to whether she'd seen some money she kept on the side into an accusation that I'd stolen it.'

'And had you?' Rafferty enquired.

'No, I bloody hadn't.' After a drumbeat's pause, with disarming candour, Jesmond added, 'Wish I had now, though.'

'So what happened next?'

'Jane went mad – mad at *me*. Jeez, you know, one minute I'm minding my own business, painting her old mother's walls 'cos Jane wants to get on her mum's right side and the next it's *my* fault that her bloody mother's forgotten where she put her money. Jane had a right go at me. Told me I had no balls if I allowed her mother to accuse me of theft and get away with it.

'By this time, with all Jane's taunts, I'd pretty well forgotten that the old girl hadn't accused *me* of theft at all. Anyway, to placate Jane, I started having a go at the old woman myself. By this time, we were out on the landing. I was still shouting at Jane's mum, though Jane had already gone quiet. Then, all of a sudden, Jane grabbed my arm, told me, loudly, to leave her mum alone, and hustled me away.'

Jesmond shook his head. 'I still don't understand what it was all about. First off, out of the blue, Jane starts a barney with her mother, gets me involved, then once I'm going full throttle, equally as suddenly, she calls a halt to the row and backs off.'

It was certainly strange – if Darryl's version of events was to be believed.

Rafferty found himself wondering if Jane had deliberately set Darryl up as her patsy to get back at him for flirting with her young daughter and for his unsubtle dalliance with the lady at the bar, who was amassing a growing collection of expensive cocktails.

Had Jane deliberately forced the argument, making it sound to the late Clara Mortimer's elderly apartment neighbours as if it was *Darryl*, not Jane, who had reason to bear a grudge against Mrs Mortimer?

What was it Amelia Frobisher had said? That she hadn't realized Jane had been in Clara Mortimer's apartment at all.

'I certainly never heard her,' she had told them. 'All I heard was that young man she lives with shouting at Clara and Clara shouting back that he was a thief. I only realized Jane was there at all when I happened to glance out of the window a few minutes later and saw her drive off in that dilapidated old car of hers, her young man beside her as she pulled out of the car park and turned on to Cymbeline Way.'

Such a setting-up of Darryl could indicate premeditation before the fact of matricide on Jane's part. Though of course, with Jane Ogilvie, it might simply indicate that she had taken umbrage that Darryl and her mother were getting on well together – even sharing the decorating duties in an amicable manner. Rafferty could see that would put irritating grit in the oyster of Jane's personality.

From Darryl Jesmond's other side, Llewellyn asked, 'And the other strange behaviour, sir?'

'What? Oh, yeah. To get back to what you said earlier about Charlie's arrival. It's funny that Jane should have tried to make a big production out of it when I'd already said the day before, when he arrived out of the blue, that he could stay for a few days. That's what I mean when I say she's been behaving oddly.'

He scowled down at his beer. 'Though given the little

bombshell she dropped earlier, it's likely her hormones are all over the place, right?'

Jesmond picked up his lager and took another huge gulp that emptied half the pint pot, before he asked plaintively, 'Is that it? Only I'd like to get my lady friend back before one of those suits at the bar makes her forget about me completely.'

Judging from the reassumed cock-of-the-walk body language and the sneer he directed at the pigeon-chested and be-suited bar-proppers, it was clear Darryl Jesmond thought the last unlikely.

It was later the next day when Llewellyn finally managed to get to speak to the imam at the local mosque.

He was thoughtful when he returned.

'I've just found out one more of Mrs Ogilvie's brood in a lie,' he said to Rafferty. 'Remember that Hakim told us he was studying at the local mosque at the time of his grandmother's murder?'

Rafferty gave the required nod to this rhetorical question and waited to see what Llewellyn's discreet enquiries had turned up.

'According to the imam, Hakim wasn't at the mosque that morning. He should have been as he has instruction regularly every week, but the imam said Hakim's interest in religion has taken a downward turn lately and he's missed a few of these instruction periods. The imam, who seems a kindly man, was of the opinion that young Hakim has discovered girls and when we questioned him he would have been too embarrassed to admit it, especially in front of his mother, whom, the imam said, young Hakim regards as a loose woman.'

Rafferty nodded. Now he thought about it, Hakim's manner had seemed unnecessarily defensive. He wondered if the imam was right and the handsome, sixteen-year-old Hakim had been doing what teenage boys had done through the centuries – trying to persuade a girl to go to bed with him.

But, as Llewellyn commented, after his condemnation of his mother for her promiscuous behaviour, he would be reluctant to admit the loss of both face and the high moral ground in front of her.

'Maybe he might be cajoled into telling the truth if I can get him on his own,' Rafferty commented. He glanced at his watch. 'Nearly school chucking-out time. I'll get over to St Vincent's and waylay the lad.'

At 3.55, Rafferty stationed himself at the gates of St Vincent's School. Little more than a minute after the nearest church bell had chimed four, he was engulfed in the middle of a swarm of bumblebee dark-brown and yellow uniforms of the youths and girls that rushed past him in their eagerness to escape the halls of learning.

Rafferty almost missed Hakim in the crush. It was only the boy's height, his proud carriage, and the desert-night darkness of his hair that enabled him to spot him amongst the drab brown-sparrow colouring of most of his schoolmates.

Jeered and heckled, promised a 'duffing-up' by one of the many overgrown youths as he pushed his way through the noisy throng in pursuit of Hakim, Rafferty just smiled and exchanged banter instead of wielding the authority of his warrant card.

Besides, he didn't fancy his chances against the boy, who towered above him and must be six foot four if he was an inch and weigh all of sixteen stone.

What on earth was modern youth being fed? Rafferty wondered, bemused as this overgrown youthful tide engulfed him. Surely a diet full of Mac-this and Mac-that couldn't be responsible for the race of giants the country seemed to be breeding?

Having managed to avoid being on the receiving end of the promised duffing-up, Rafferty caught up with Hakim, who walked alone, apart from the little bevy of teenage girls who followed just behind and who were egging one another on to approach the boy.

Hakim, Rafferty noticed as he fell into step beside him, simply ignored the girls and their giggling. The teenager gave him one startled glance before his long-lashed eyelids swooped down as swiftly as a bird of prey over his amazing golden eyes.

'Remember telling me you were at the mosque at the time your grandmother died?' Rafferty remarked conversationally when they had finally put some distance between themselves and Hakim's lovelorn female fans.

Hakim gave him a wary, sideways glance and just nodded.

'Then you won't be surprised that we've learned you weren't at the mosque at all.'

Rafferty wondered if Hakim had expected the imam to lie for him to Llewellyn, the infidel; if so, he was doubly shamed – for lying and being caught lying. No wonder Hakim's high-cheekboned face took on a glowing red tinge that made him look even more broodingly handsome.

'I suppose you were with a girl?'

When this question met with no response, Rafferty added, 'OK, I can understand that you didn't want to say so in front of your mother, but your mother's not here now. So, come on – where were you really?'

Hakim shot him a sideways glance of pure hatred, but still chose to say nothing.

'Good-looking lad like you must have your pick of the girls,' Rafferty observed, 'judging from the fan club behind us.'

This fan club had found sufficient bravado to coo after Hakim, 'Hakim, we love you,' much to this young man's barely concealed mortification.

'So which one's your girlfriend?' Rafferty persisted. 'My guess would be the pretty little blonde.'

His guess only elicited a scornful sneer.

'You might as well tell me,' he went on, 'because once we start asking questions, it doesn't generally take long for the answers to come out.'

His expression sullen, Hakim seemed to acknowledge the truth of this statement. After a few moments' more struggle, he supplied his girlfriend's name.

To Rafferty's surprise, rather than one of his pretty school-mates, Hakim's preferred girlfriend turned out to be one of his neighbours, one Julie – or 'Jules' as she preferred to call herself – Kirkland.

Jules Kirkland had more mature charms than the pretty little blonde that Rafferty had thought more likely to appeal to the handsome Hakim.

But when Rafferty managed to dredge her statement up from his memory of the many statements he had read, he realized that Jules Kirkland had been the only one of the neighbourhood adults *not* to have a down on Hakim. Now, he understood just why that should be.

Sixteen-year-old Hakim glanced sideways and said, 'You seem surprised that I should prefer a mature woman to these silly young girls. But what can they teach a boy? If I was in my father's country, he would have already arranged for me to learn from an older woman how to become a skilful lover to spare me the shameful fumblings that pass for love-making in this country.'

Ouch! Rafferty thought as he recalled some of his own shameful youthful fumbling. An older woman would certainly have come in handy then, he thought ruefully.

'And you were with this Jules Kirkland around seven on the morning of your grandmother's death?'

'Do not call her that,' Hakim immediately flared at him. 'She refused to acknowledge me as her grandson. Equally, I will not recognize her as my grandmother.'

'Yes, well, that aside for the moment – were you with this Jules Kirkland on that morning? Yes or no?' Rafferty repeated.

At Rafferty's subtle re-phrasing, Hakim supplied a tight-lipped 'Yes,' before his youth betrayed him and he asked Rafferty anxiously, 'You won't tell my mother, will you? Only . . . Only . . .'

Only the moral high ground will be pulled from under me, Rafferty guessed was what Hakim wanted to say, but what his pride wouldn't allow him to admit.

Given Hakim's understandable sensitivity about his father's failure to acknowledge him, his determined pride in his half-Arabic parenthood and his shame that the promiscuous Jane should be his mother, Rafferty felt a moment's pity for the teenager's obvious turmoil.

'Don't worry,' he assured the youth. 'As long as this Ms Kirkland backs you up, I can't see why your mother should have to know anything at all about it.'

From his expression, Hakim seemed split between acknowledging Rafferty's sensitivity and defending his honour after being found out in a lie.

Rafferty, recalling his own childhood's tortured Catholic experience of sexual matters, patted Hakim on the shoulder and went off to question Jules Kirkand before Hakim felt obliged to bruise his honour further by voicing either reluctant thanks or churlish affront.

Twelve

After all the lies and evasions of Jane Ogilvie, her boyfriend, father and children, Rafferty set out that evening after work looking forward to the refreshing, uncomplicated task of doing his babysitting stint. Compared to his demanding day job, he felt confident the babysitting would be a doddle.

With Gemma and her baby now out of hospital and back home with her mother, the much-anticipated evening of the boy band's concert had arrived.

Rafferty, determined to put things right between himself and Abra, determined also to prove his worth as a potential daddy via his female family members' grapevine, had beaten off all childminding challengers.

He turned up bright and early for his babysitting duties. In case Gemma had come over all eco-friendly on the nappy front and decided to use terries instead of the easier disposables, he'd even equipped himself with an instruction book written for new fathers which distilled wisdom on the nappy-folding, croup-curing and sleep-inducing fronts. Confident he'd covered all angles, Rafferty walked up the path and knocked on his sister's front door.

Maggie greeted his appearance with a doubtful expression. 'Are you sure you understand what you're letting yourself in for, Joe?' she asked as she took in the smart jacket and freshly laundered white shirt that Rafferty had deemed appropriate wear for babysitting. 'I didn't expect Mum to get Gemma and her friend tickets for this boy band for the same night Frank and I had arranged to go to an anniversary party. We don't *have* to go, of course . . .'

'Don't be daft, Maggie-May. I can't have my sister all dressed up, pretty as a picture and going nowhere.'

It was true his sister looked a treat in a strappy rich-turquoise dress that emphasized the colour of her eyes. Her raven hair, piled loosely on top of her head, had tendrils trailing down. Altogether, she looked a knockout. Given that she rarely had an opportunity to dress up and enjoy herself, Rafferty wasn't about to be the cause of her cancelling a much-looked-forward-to evening.

'Well if you're sure . . . ?'

'I'm as sure as I'm sure I'm still standing here. Can I come in or am I to do my childminding stint from the doorstep?'

Maggie laughed. 'Idiot. Come in. The brats are all home,' she warned. 'Don't let them stay up too late.'

The eldest of Rafferty's three younger sisters had followed their mother's fecund childbearing example, though Maggie had stopped at four. At sixteen, Gemma was her eldest and the only girl.

Rafferty received an enthusiastic welcome from his nephews especially when they discovered he'd brought the latest fantasy film with him. Gemma was nowhere to be seen. He asked where she was.

'Where do you think? She's upstairs making herself beautiful for Ciaran Prenderghast,' Maggie told him. 'Now, let's get you sorted. I've left the phone number of our friends on the hall table. Call me if you have any problems.'

Maggie led him into the kitchen. She showed him the made-up bottles for the baby, the gripe water, the nappies – terries – all ready folded into their kites much to his relief, as, in spite of the book that promised to instil wisdom in such matters, he hadn't had time to completely get to grips with the complexities of nappy-folding. She explained how to heat the milk and how to make sure it wasn't too hot.

'Oh, and don't—' she began before Rafferty cut her off. 'Maggie, stop fussing. He's only a baby. How hard can it be?'

Shortly after, Frank, Maggie's husband, came bustling in, shouted Gemma away from her mirror and hurried the two women out the front door.

Maggie cast one last, anxious look behind her, which caused Rafferty to shout reassuringly, 'Don't worry. We'll be fine. Be off with you and have a great evening, the lot of you.'

It was only five minutes later, after Rafferty had sat down between his nephews and settled back to enjoy the new film, when he recognized the piercing cries of his great-nephew.

Thirty minutes later, the baby was still going strong. His three nephews had long since decamped upstairs, taking the latest film with them. He could make out the title music booming down the stairs as a block on baby nephew noise.

Rafferty bounced the baby up and down. He gurgled at him. Made faces at him. Shifted him from one arm to the other. Nothing shut him up.

He decided the child must be hungry and heated one of the prepared bottles. But when he tried to feed him, his great-nephew spurned his offer with indignant fury.

Nappy-changing was equally unsuccessful – at least from Rafferty's point of view – though the baby would certainly have pleased the advertisers currently proclaiming the containment properties of their eco-friendly terries. Perhaps if Rafferty hadn't interrupted proceedings, the nappies *would*, as they proudly boasted, have contained the baby's emissions . . .

Why hadn't his sister warned him that the baby had the runs and could aim a deadly-accurate stream of shit from a yard away? he wondered as with his free hand, he eased off his pebble-dashed once-white shirt.

He laid the baby down in the corner of the settee on top of another couple of freshly laundered nappies while he went upstairs to have a quick shower and to search for a clean shirt in Frank's wardrobe.

He had hoped the baby might have dozed off in the interim. But there was to be no such luck, he realized, as he came downstairs and heard the baby still going at full-throttle above the noise of his nephews' film.

He still smelt faintly of baby shit; he wondered if the kid had a bellyache. After wrestling the wriggling baby into another nappy, he decided to try him on the gripe water his sister had so thoughtfully left on the kitchen table.

Ten minutes and much frustration later, exasperation had begun to set in. The gripe water had failed to restore the desired sound of silence. Rafferty and the now red-faced baby tried out-staring one another. The baby won.

'Gemma's going to have her hands full with you, isn't she? Rambo, or whatever she's decided to call you,' he remarked.

The baby replied with an even more ear-piercing crescendo of screams. More emissions escaped Rafferty's amateurishly applied nappy. Then he had a brainwave. Hadn't his ma confessed she'd sometimes had recourse to desperate measures when he or one of his five siblings wouldn't sleep?

He patted his pocket and brought out a slim metal flask. Luckily he'd brought the necessary with him: with three sons in their teens or near as damn it, his brother-in-law kept his booze firmly locked away, as Rafferty had had occasion to discover in the past.

'This'll get you off,' he promised the baby. 'It always works a treat on me.'

He warmed the milk up again, then tipped some out to accommodate the Jameson's whisky, before he screwed the teat back on.

The baby proved he had his full complement of Rafferty

genes because this time he sucked the laced milk with a true toper's enthusiasm. Five minutes' later, congratulating himself on his babysitting skills, a blissfully peaceful Rafferty, thankfully with an even more blissfully sleeping baby in his arms, slumped back on the settee. Game, set and match to me, I think, he told the now sleep-smiling baby triumphantly.

Rafferty decided he deserved something soothing even more than the baby did. And after two large ones he was feeling pleasantly relaxed. Wary of carrying the baby upstairs to his cot in case the jarring disturbed him, Rafferty eased him into the carrycot and put him in the dark and quiet of the kitchen before he sneaked on tiptoe back to the living room. He turned the volume down before turning on the TV and was just in time to catch the beginning of the film on Channel 5.

He settled down to watch, but after twenty minutes, he concluded the film wasn't one of their better offerings and decided that his rumbling stomach was more deserving of attention.

A chip butty was in order, he thought as he crept into the darkened kitchen. He didn't want to put on the light and so disturb the mercifully sleeping baby, but he needed to find the chip pan. He lit the gas and, using the illumination this provided, he looked around his sister's small kitchen for the chip pan; he found it on a high shelf above the cooker.

He dragged a stool out from under the kitchen table, climbed up and reached for the pan. It was only as he tugged at the chip pan that he realized something was lodged on top of it, which his tugging at the chip pan sent flying.

Fearing a clatter that would waken the sleeping baby, Rafferty essayed a pirouette, à la Rudolph Nureyev in his heyday. Alas – not being a Nureyev, heyday or otherwise – he not only missed the flying pan lid, but managed – with the fear uppermost in his mind of landing on the sleeping baby – to somehow twist his body in mid-air and land chest-first on the still-burning gas ring.

Smouldering, with the smell of burnt hair and roasted flesh wafting up his nostrils, Rafferty winced and turned off the gas. After checking that, by some miracle, the baby still slept, he rushed upstairs and, for the second time that evening, washed off the damage under his sister's shower.

It was only after the sting of the burns on his chest began to wane under the cold water that the uneasy certainty struck him that the shirt he had earlier so cavalierly borrowed from Frank's wardrobe had been his brother-in-law's favourite. Now, between burn holes and baby shit, it was completely ruined.

As Rafferty dried himself, put his clothes back on and borrowed another shirt from his brother-in-law's fast-diminishing wardrobe, he wondered what excuse he could come up with for the burnt offerings that constituted Frank's favourite shirt.

It was only much later than evening as he heard the key in the door and knew that his sister, Frank and Gemma had returned, that he realized coming up with a believable excuse for the funeral pyre he had made of Frank's best shirt was beyond him. It would be better for his brother-in-law to think the shirt had made one of those mysterious bids for freedom to which laundry was prone, he thought, as he stuffed it to the bottom of the carrier bag beneath his New Man babysitting book of wisdom.

Gemma, all starry-eyed and even more in love with the lead singer of the boy band, suffered a rush back to reality when Rafferty told her the baby was sound asleep in the kitchen.

'Oh, Uncle Joe,' she complained, as Rafferty's acrobatically gained and heroic burns stung afresh and unsung. 'Why didn't you put him to bed?'

'I was frightened of disturbing him once I'd got him off,' he defensively explained.

Gemma pulled a face. 'That means *I'll* have to do it. I bet he'll wake up and not go off again.'

'Don't be so ungrateful, Gemma,' Maggie admonished her pouting daughter. 'Your uncle Joe was good enough to babysit so you could go out. I think you should be thanking him rather than moaning at him.'

Rafferty, whose offer to babysit had sprung from the far from selfless ulterior motive of getting back in Abra's good books, flushed a bit at this. Fortunately, neither Gemma nor Maggie suspected this. Even more fortunately, the whisky proved its worth and the young Rambo or whatever Gemma decided to call him didn't stir when Gemma picked him up and took him upstairs to his cot. The boys had long since gone to bed.

'Isn't it about time you decided on a name for the child?' Rafferty asked when Gemma came back downstairs, a few minutes' later.

'Suppose so. If I'd had a girl I was set on calling her Britney or Beyoncé,' she said. 'But as it's a boy, I'm thinking of Ciaran or Damon.'

Rafferty bit back the grimace. But he couldn't restrain the thought – as if being a fatherless ginger nut wasn't enough for the poor little tyke without saddling him with some boy band member's nancified name.

Wary of encouraging her to dig her heels in, Rafferty said, 'Of course, it's up to you, sweetheart, but think about a few years down the line when that singer's been bounced out of the charts by the latest pop sensation. Do you really want your son to be left with the name of a pop has-been?'

Gemma's expression exuded uncertainty; clearly, between the desire to chastize her uncle for speaking such a heresy about her faultless hero and her new mother's desire to do the best for her son, she was undecided which way to jump.

Rafferty thought a gentle push towards the latter option was odds-on favourite.

He tried a careless laugh. 'I remember I was at school with a boy named Elvis Jones. He was the dullest stick you ever met. Couldn't dance or sing to save his life and went bald in his twenties. He became an accountant. Not a very successful one. I mean, can there be many people prepared to place their financial well-being in the hands of an accountant called Elvis?

'No one knows how their kid's going to turn out or what they might become. I always think it's doing a kid a kindness to stick to names that have stood the test of time.'

'Like Joseph, you mean?' Gemma asked dryly.

Relieved to see that, for all her new burdens, his young niece retained the capacity to tease, he agreed. 'Joseph's certainly stood the test of time. So take *your* time, Gemma, but choose like a wise parent.'

He thought of Jane Ogilvie and her resentment of the name that had brought years of playground teasing. It provided him with fresh ammunition.

'If you don't want your son resenting you and your choice into middle age and beyond, just remember Elvis the unsuccessful accountant. Imagine what he must have thought of *his* parents.'

Feeling he'd done a good evening's duties on both the babysitting and Dutch Uncle fronts, Rafferty said his goodnights, left his car where it was till the morning and walked home.

The next day Ma rang Rafferty at work just before he left the station and invited – no, *insisted* he take a detour to her house before he went home.

Puzzled, but resigned, Rafferty, who didn't feel up to falling out with the other main woman in his life, decided that eating one of his ma's home-cooked dinners was an easier option than refusing her invitation.

Only, when he arrived at his ma's home, he wasn't met by the looked-forward-to waft of appetizing aromas. He followed his ma through to the kitchen and glanced at the oven light as she filled the kettle – nothing. He checked the dial – ditto. Reluctantly, he concluded that if something was cooking, it certainly wasn't dinner, which had to be a first for ma, who always practically force-fed her visitors. Even if you said no thanks, she always kept on until you agreed to a sandwich at least.

Scenting trouble rather than a nice casserole with rhubarb crumble and custard to follow, Rafferty asked plaintively, 'So, what's up, Ma? Is your plumbing playing up again? Have you got a leaky stopcock you want me to fix?'

'It's not me with the leaky stopcock, from what I've observed, Joseph,' his ma replied as she thumped the kettle on the gas ring and lit it.

Rafferty wasn't a detective for nothing. The thumped kettle, the use of his full given name and the comment about 'leaks' and 'cocks', provided clues in plenty, even for an Inspector Clouseau.

With justification, suspecting where the conversation was heading, he prevaricated. 'What are you on about, Ma?'

'Joseph. I wasn't born yesterday, so don't carry on as if I was.'

His ma pulled two mugs off their hooks, placed them on a tray on the cheap, blue Formica table, took a bottle of milk from the fridge and decanted it into a small cream jug, before she turned to face him.

'Unless I've misread the signs – which I doubt, since I've carried six babies to term – your Abra's pregnant.'

Rafferty opened his mouth to deny it. But as he realized that denial was futile, he shut it again.

'Well might you make like a stranded fish. What were you thinking of?' she asked as the kettle boiled and she warmed the teapot. 'Surely, at your age, you've learned about contraception?'

Although staunch in her Catholic faith, contraception was one of those subjects on which his ma's path diverged from the Pope's; but then she had never been one unthinkingly to follow his lead in everything. He was a man, after all, was her reasoning, so even *he* couldn't be right all the time. And on this particular subject, he was a man of no experience whatever. As she had frequently had occasion to remark, when Rafferty and his five siblings had been young and were being particularly troublesome, if she had had more than the rhythm method and the 'No' word to rely on, several little Raffertys wouldn't have been born at all.

He was about to explain about Abra's gastric attack, but his ma cut off his explanation.

'So – *are* we to have another illegitimate baby in the family?' she asked, as, under her breath, she added, 'As if young Gemma's boy isn't one illegitimate child too far.'

Rafferty gained a brief respite while the tea-making distracted her. He made use of the time to think furiously. Unfortunately, the ten seconds required for tea-making were never going to be long enough for him to come up with worthy self-defence measures.

She thrust the tea tray at him. 'You can take that through. I'll bring the pot.'

Rafferty did as ordered. No biscuits, he noticed. He must really be in his ma's bad books. And seeing as his ma had shown she was au fait with his 'secret', he supposed he might as well come clean. Honesty might gain him a few brownie points.

So when they had sat down in Ma's living room, Rafferty said, 'All right. I admit it. Abra thinks she might be pregnant. But it's not my fault—'

His ma nearly choked on her tea at this statement. Kitty Rafferty – who had a flexible mind on legal matters – wasn't nearly so elastic in matters moral and had never, as he knew from previous experience, been one to lightly permit denial of responsibility.

And as she thumped her mug down on the side table, she demanded tartly, 'So whose fault is it, then? God's? The

Archangel Gabriel's? What exactly are you trying to say, Joseph? That it's going to be a second virgin birth? Or that the baby's not yours?'

'Neither. Of course, neither.'

'I suppose I must be thankful for small mercies.'

'All I'm saying,' he explained when he finally managed to put forward his excuse, 'is that Abra suffered a gastric attack shortly before we—'

'Yes, thank you, Joseph. I don't need the eldest of my six children explaining to me how babies are made.' She sighed and shook her head. 'Surely you knew the pill's not to be relied on when the woman's stomach's upset?' which – as Abra's suspected pregnancy provided its own answer – didn't require further substantiation from Rafferty.

He brought in his reserves. 'Anyway, I'm not even sure there *is* a baby.'

He explained about Abra's refusal to take a pregnancy test.

His ma's expression told him she suspected he had handled the conversation with all the finesse of a drunken Irishman. But as he'd had a few drinks that lunchtime and was Irish on both sides, that was scarcely his fault.

'Pregnancy tests – didn't need such things in my young day.' Tentatively – as if she feared more choking revelations – his ma took another sip of her tea. 'A woman should know her own body – that's far more reliable than any pregnancy test. Anyway, you can take it from me, my lad, Abra *is* expecting. She had all the signs when I saw her last week; nearly two months along, if I'm any judge.'

With that forward thrust of her chin that Rafferty recognized of old, together with the determined glint in her eye, she demanded, 'So what are you going to do about it?'

As Rafferty recalled that his ma had been robbed of a family wedding when young Wayne Newson, Gemma's ex-boyfriend and the father of her new son, had refused to do the decent thing, he couldn't help but wonder if he was

about to be 'persuaded' into the second shotgun wedding
of his life. Not that he would be sorry, if so. Unlike his first
shotgun marriage, he would marry Abra and gladly. The
only difficulties would be getting Abra to listen to, never
mind accept, his proposal and then turn up for the ceremony . . .

'I don't know *what* to do about it,' Rafferty admitted.
'Abra won't talk to me. Now don't look at me like that,
Ma,' he warned. 'I admit I didn't react that well when Abra
told me she thought she was pregnant. But her announce-
ment *did* come out of the blue. She landed it in my lap
without any kind of warning and then got upset because I
didn't immediately get on to Mothercare and start ordering
Babygros by the lorry-load.'

Glumly, he added, 'And now, as I said, she won't even
return my phone calls. So I don't know what I'm going to
do. I wish I did.'

Quietly, she asked, 'Do you want the baby?'

'Yes. No. Maybe.' Rafferty was astonished to find
himself, in his answers, echoing Abra. He shrugged, added,
'I don't know. Abra didn't even give me a chance to get
used to the idea before she tore into me. I really don't know
what to do for the best. And even if I *did*, what can I do
when Abra refuses to talk to me? I get the impression I
could propose marriage down on both knees with the red
rose of romance clenched between my cheeks and I'd still
get the bum's rush.'

'Language, Joseph.'

His ma poured them both a second cup of tea, told him
to fetch the biscuits and turn the oven on, while she pondered
his predicament.

When he returned from his kitchen duties, he found his
ma sipping slowly on her now cooled tea. Between sips,
she told him, 'Your trouble, son, is that you don't understand women. It's quite amazing really, given that you've
a mother, three sisters, nieces and female cousins beyond

counting. Fortunately, for you, I *do* understand the female mind.'

She set her mug down on the side table and leant forward decisively. 'Now here's what I suggest you do.'

Thirteen

Rafferty had taken his ma's advice on board and bombarded Abra with deliveries of flowers, wine, chocolates and humble petitions in equal proportions. But she was *still* ignoring him. Maybe if he—

'Quiet times?'

Rafferty broke off from his reverie at Llewellyn's comment.

'What?' he asked.

Llewellyn sat down on the opposite side of the table in the police canteen. In front of him, with unnecessary tentativeness, he placed a healthy salad baguette and a plastic tumbler filled with what looked like grapefruit juice.

Rafferty pulled a face at this last item. How anyone could drink such bitter stuff . . . ?

It was a late lunch for both of them. It was almost 3.00 p.m., apart from the canteen staff, himself and Llewellyn, the canteen was almost empty.

'It's just that you've been rather introspective lately,' Llewellyn remarked. He picked up the baguette but didn't bite into it. 'I wondered if there was anything amiss.' Llewellyn hesitated before he asked, with a degree of bluntness that was usually foreign to him, 'You're not in trouble again, are you?'

Llewellyn was referring to the dilemma Rafferty had experienced back in April shortly before Llewellyn had introduced him to Abra, when he had risked having his collar felt and going down for a long stretch.

'No,' Rafferty was quick to reassure. 'I'm not in the sort of trouble you mean.'

Delicately, Llewellyn put his baguette back on its plate. 'But your answer indicates trouble of some sort. Care to tell me about it?'

Clearly, his sergeant suspected he was going to have to pull Rafferty's coals out of the fire again.

Llewellyn's sensitive interrogation earned him a noncommittal shrug. There were no flies on Llewellyn, Rafferty conceded. But then, as Llewellyn had just pointed out, since he had more or less admitted to trouble of some sort, there didn't need to be.

'Abra all right?'

'Yes,' was Rafferty's brusque reply. As far as *he* knew, he thought. It was a thought he didn't vocalize, but he couldn't keep back the sharp question. 'Why do you ask?' Had Llewellyn heard something? he wondered. 'Have you heard something?' he asked eagerly. Too eagerly?

Llewellyn's next words reassured him about this at least.

'No. Why? What should I have heard?'

'Nothing. Of course, nothing.'

Llewellyn frowned, first at Rafferty, then down at his untouched baguette. 'It's strange now I think of it, but Abra hasn't been in contact for some days. It's not like her. I got no answer when I tried to ring her.'

Join the club, thought Rafferty. He supposed it was some consolation to discover he wasn't the only male in Abra's life who was getting the silent treatment. Though in Llewellyn's case, Abra's lack of communication wasn't surprising, given that she believed herself pregnant. With Llewellyn and Maureen trying – and so far, failing – to conceive, Abra was unlikely to turn to her cousin and his wife if she wanted a shoulder to cry on.

Llewellyn took a sip of his juice before he observed, 'It's unusual for her to leave more than a day or two between phone calls.'

Rafferty replaced his knife and fork on his plate with a clatter. His fry-up was already congealing. He'd gone off it anyway. 'And your first thought was that I must have done something to upset her?'

Llewellyn looked taken aback at this accusation. 'No. Of course not.' Above his dark, Welsh eyes, his brows raised interrogatively. 'Why would I think such a thing?'

Rafferty felt the intellectual Llewellyn's scrutiny dissecting him like a kipper. 'Look', he grunted. 'We've had a row. All right? That's all. A row. Don't you and Maureen have rows?'

Llewellyn's expression became thoughtful as he pondered this, before he said, 'We have discussions, certainly. I don't know whether you'd call them rows exactly.'

Rafferty nodded gloomily at this. He couldn't imagine the emotionally cool Welshman having a right upper and downer with the intellectual bluestocking, Maureen.

Llewellyn's head nodded towards Rafferty's abandoned fry-up. 'The row was obviously serious enough to put you off your food. Care to talk about it?'

'No.'

Rebuffed, Llewellyn picked up his baguette again and took a bite.

They sat for several minutes in silence while Llewellyn chewed his way to the end of his lunch. Then he again gestured at Rafferty's barely touched meal and said, 'If you're not going to eat that, perhaps we ought to head for Parkview Apartments? You said you wanted to speak to the other residents again. Unless—?'

'The residents will have to wait a bit,' Rafferty informed Llewellyn as he jerked his chair back from the table with a teeth-clenching screech. 'I've got to go out. Private business,' he briefly explained. 'I shouldn't be any more than twenty minutes or so.' Unless he struck lucky, that was. 'Wait for me.'

*   *   *

For the third time in a day and a half, Rafferty stood on the doorstep to Abra's apartment block and rang the bell. And for the third time he received no response.

Frustrated, this time he tried ringing one of her neighbour's doorbells. When he again got no response, he rang a second, then a third, before he finally got one of Abra's neighbours to answer.

'Police,' he grunted down the intercom. 'I'm checking on Ms Abra Kearney.'

'Why?' The disembodied northern voice demanded in the not-backward-in-coming-forward manner in which all true Yorkshire folk took a positive pride. 'What's she done?'

'She hasn't done anything, sir. Someone's reported her missing.'

They hadn't, of course, but it was something Rafferty was seriously considering. From his point of view, the situation was getting desperate.

Not that reporting a grown woman missing was likely to raise the hue and cry or even winkle Abra out from wherever she was currently concealing herself. But at least it would provide him with a ready excuse to use official means to track her down.

'Now you mention it, I haven't seen her myself for a few days, though I've seen the local florist several times.'

The spectre of complaint was clearly discernible in the Yorkshireman's tone.

'There's a veritable funeral parlour of floral tributes sitting outside her door,' the man confided. 'Not to mention other deliveries. They're cluttering up the corridor. Makes you wonder if she's got some deranged stalker after her.'

The man's flat accent rose several bars up the scale as excitement took a grip.

'Do you think something's happened to her, then?' he asked. 'I know she's got a boyfriend,' the neighbour confided again. 'I only got a glimpse of him the once. Back end of April it would have been. But he certainly looked thuggish enough to be capable of anything.'

Rafferty grimaced. He had heard too many similar comments about his appearance back in April to appreciate one more. Nice to have the neighbour's vote of confidence, he thought, though he had to concede that the man had a point. Because at the back end of April he had still been waiting for his number one haircut to grow back, so, no doubt, he had merited the 'thuggish' description of Abra's neighbour.

This brief feeling of empathy vanished at the man's next words.

With a thrill in his voice, the neighbour asked breathlessly, 'Do you think he's *killed* her?'

'No. Certainly not.'

From the silence that followed Rafferty's perhaps over-hasty denial, he guessed that the man was fighting a battle with the desire for celebrity. If so, it was a brief battle. He had reached no more than a count of three in what was no doubt an unequal struggle before the man threw in the towel to demand:

'Ooh – will I be on that crime programme on the telly?'

Disgusted, Rafferty crushed the would-be telly-celebrity's hopes for his fifteen minutes of fame. 'We have no reason to believe anything's happened to Ms Kearney,' he tersely replied.

Disappointment replaced the thrill. And was as rapidly followed by disgruntlement as if Abra's concerned neighbour thought Rafferty had deliberately deceived him.

'Then why are you looking for her?' he demanded brusquely. 'You've already said she hasn't done anything to interest the police. Now you say you've no reason to suspect she's at any sort of risk.'

The voice performed another descant up the scales. 'Haven't the police got anything better to do with my taxes than chase after a grown woman for no good reason? With all the crime—'

Rafferty cut him off in mid-sentence. 'We have our reasons, sir,' he told the intercom. 'But thank you for your concern. I'll be sure to tell Ms Kearney about it when I locate her. She'll find it a comfort to know she has a neighbour with such community spirit.'

Abra's neighbour must have had some semblance of shame, for after Rafferty's tart comment, he slammed the receiver down with a crash.

Now what? Rafferty thought, as, back in the car, he considered his options. The consideration of these didn't take long. His ma's suggested floral bombardment hadn't worked. How could it when it was clear that Abra wasn't at her flat? The same applied to his other wallet-emptying gifts and his endless phone messages.

As far as he could see, he didn't *have* any options beyond reporting her missing. While Abra was determined to continue her vanishing act, all the options were hers.

But, in the meantime, he still had a murder to solve . . .

So he drove back to the station. And as his brain clicked back into 'official' mode, he recalled Llewellyn's reminder that they were meant to be conducting follow-up interviews with the late Clara Mortimer's fellow Parkview residents.

In his present mood, Rafferty felt little inclination to sit through a second re-enactment of the 'Mat Wars' of Rita Atkins and Amelia Frobisher. But, as he had already concluded with regard to his love life, this was an arena where choice wasn't in his bailiwick.

He glanced at his watch and was surprised to find it was after four o'clock. He headed for the station. No doubt Llewellyn would be there waiting for him, champing at the bit to get on with the investigation and with more 'Abra' questions that Rafferty was unable to answer.

As he drove past Elmhurst's thirteenth-century market cross with its usual aimless gang of jostling teenagers, Rafferty recognized Aurora Mortimer in the centre of the throng.

Like half the group, Aurora still wore her school uniform and had a heavy school bag at her feet, which told Rafferty she had not been home. But when he thought about her home, he couldn't blame her for preferring to hang around the streets instead.

In the brief seconds as he passed, he caught a freeze-frame moment of Aurora Mortimer's life; a bevy of aggressively shoulder-thrusting local youths surrounded her, their expressions hungry as they competed for the attentions of the exotic Aurora.

Even in such a limited out-take from Aurora's life it was clear that, unlike her mother, Aurora would always be in control. Not for *her* her mother's foolish, blundering rebellion again the control of others which merely meant the controller's identity, rather than the situation, changed.

It was apparent the young Aurora had the local males exactly where she wanted them. Her stance, with her gaze directed beyond the youths, said they would do until a male more worthy of her came along.

Rafferty could only hope, for Aurora Mortimer's sake, that she didn't decide this more worthy male was Darryl Jesmond.

Rafferty picked up Llewellyn at the police station and, with the Welshman's body still emitting curiosity in silent waves, they headed for the station car park.

To avoid the voicing of these thus far mercifully silent questions, Rafferty roared away from the Bacon Lane back entrance to the police station with what he hoped was sufficient turbo-thrust to render Llewellyn speechless as the G-forces encouraged his tongue to dance a tango with his tonsils.

When he and Llewellyn arrived at the Parkview sheltered apartments, it was to find the residents gathered in reception, in the process of having a meeting to discuss the block's security.

As soon as they entered, Rafferty heard Amelia Frobisher's piercing voice; it drowned out the voices and opinions of the other residents. When she spotted Rafferty, she surged through the gathered residents like a battle-trimmed galleon with all her befrilled pennants flying and buttonholed him.

'Inspector,' she trilled. 'We've just been discussing how best to increase our security in view of the attack on poor dear Clara.'

Rafferty noted her delicate reluctance to use the word 'murder'.

'Perhaps, Inspector,' Amelia Frobisher went on, 'we could ask you for some advice?'

Rafferty was unwillingly put on the spot; he had already concluded that the security measures at the sheltered apartments were excellent – certainly, the security was far superior to anything that most people had. And given that the evidence pointed to Clara Mortimer being killed by someone who knew her, then, clearly, it was an 'inside' job and no amount of security could have made a scrap of difference.

Reluctantly, he turned to face his interlocutor. Resisting the urge to throw off the bony but persistent and surprisingly strong grip that Amelia Frobisher had on his arm, he said, 'Maybe you should consider installing a camera? Of course, you would need to appoint an operator or organize a schedule for residents to replace the film and so on, and it would be expensive, but—'

'What a wonderful idea,' Amelia Frobisher gushed. 'Why didn't we think of that?' she demanded of her fellow residents.

'We did.' In a barely heard monotone, Rita Atkins added, 'But as it seems pretty certain that Mrs Mortimer wasn't murdered by an outsider, even if we'd had the camera, she'd still be dead.'

'Dear Rita,' Miss Frobisher trilled frostily. 'Must you be quite so blunt?'

Rita Atkins shrugged. 'Blunt? Call it that if you like. I call it facing reality. I don't understand why you seem so reluctant to do that.'

A hectic flush suffused Amelia Frobisher's thin features. Rita Atkins's remark seemed to have hit a sensitive spot.

But as Rafferty recalled the impressive collection of invitations with which Amelia Frobisher adorned her mantelpiece, he wondered if Rita Atkins, like himself, suspected that the invitations had been purchased and inscribed by Amelia herself. Was Rita, in retaliation for Amelia's condescension, getting her own back with the well-aimed dig?

I might only be the lowly warden, she seemed to be saying, but I don't have to stoop to sending myself fake invitations to non-existent family events.

Mrs Atkins turned to Rafferty. 'It's true though, isn't it, Inspector? That Clara Mortimer wouldn't have been saved if we'd had a camera videoing everyone who approached the entrance?'

Reluctant to agree and betray in which direction his suspicions were heading – although Rita Atkins, for one, apparently had no trouble following the clues – Rafferty merely remarked, 'As to that, I'd rather wait till we've made an arrest before I commit myself.'

Amelia Frobisher rallied and enquired crisply, 'And are you any nearer to making an arrest, Inspector?'

Her manner irritated him. Clearly, police inspectors were on a par with sheltered housing wardens in Amelia Frobisher's world.

Fortunately, just then, Rafferty's brain thrust a timely and previously unconsidered clue to the forefront of his mind. It brought an immediate surge of confidence and to the surprise of Llewellyn, he replied boldly to Amelia Frobisher's enquiry.

'We're not far from making an arrest,' he assured her.

This remark caused much excited speculative chatter and many exchanged glances amongst the gathered anxious residents, most of whom stared appraisingly at him as if doubtful whether to believe him or not.

But as he thought further on this newly revealed clue, Rafferty began to feel more confident he was at last on the right trail. After all, as Mrs Atkins had so bluntly pointed out, the evidence indicated that Clara Mortimer's murderer was someone she knew. And as Mrs Mortimer had been a solitary, reserved woman, her personal acquaintances formed a limited circle . . .

The thought brought the reminder that he had yet to re-interview Freddie Talbot. And in spite of Amelia Frobisher's claim that Talbot had been seen hanging round the apartment block for several early mornings in a row, Rafferty was unable to shrug off the suspicion that Miss Frobisher's reporting of same held more than a smidgeon of jealous spite.

Although Amelia Frobisher nodded as if satisfied by his conviction that an early arrest was on the cards, to his surprise, she failed to question him further. For once, she had little to say for herself and allowed the conversation to continue without her supplying the main contribution or guiding it the way she wanted it to go.

Rafferty found himself wondering if, after her revelations about Talbot's early-morning appearances at the apartment block, she was eagerly anticipating his arrest. Amelia Frobisher had certainly done her best to make them suspicious of the man. Talbot's vanity alone would increase the suspicion that his humiliating and public rejection by Clara Mortimer in the apartment lobby should encourage a desire for revenge on the woman who had caused the humiliation.

Harry Mortimer seemed equally subdued. It wasn't until Rafferty and Llewellyn had accompanied him in the lift to his third-floor apartment at Mortimer's request, that they learned the reason for Mortimer's subdued mien.

Rafferty discovered it was his turn to be surprised.

'I can't go on any more,' Mortimer told them. 'I've decided to own up. I killed Clara.'

Fourteen

In spite of the serious nature of his revelation, Hal Mortimer's lips parted in a wry smile and he said, 'Just another squalid little domestic, Inspector. I'm afraid it won't bring you much glory.'

He turned towards the door of his living room and asked, 'Should I pack a bag?'

Puzzled, Rafferty held up a hand. 'Hold on a minute.'

What had prompted this confession? he wondered. Surely, his own over-confident assertion in the apartments' reception area that he shortly expected to make an arrest wouldn't have seriously rattled a man like Mortimer?

'This is all a bit sudden, isn't it?' he asked. 'Why have you decided to confess now? Why not before?'

Mortimer hesitated for a moment. Then he explained with a sudden, deprecating smile that as quickly faded, 'Let's just say I'm no better at doing the right thing than the next man, Inspector. But, wouldn't you say it's better to do the right thing late rather than never?'

Rafferty – given his own failure to 'do the right thing' by Abra and the baby – shifted uncomfortably at this last statement. But as Mortimer continued, he didn't have time to examine the statement for hidden meanings.

'I've spent a lifetime seeing my family suffer because of my actions.' Mortimer shrugged. 'I suppose I just felt it was time I held my hands up and faced up to my responsibilities.' He paused. 'It's funny, when I think I've spent a lifetime wriggling out of responsibility and leaving others to carry the can. You can only wriggle for so long, I suppose, and this is one responsibility I can't dump on others.

'Now,' he added, in a surprisingly upbeat tone, 'you didn't say – but should I pack that bag?'

Rafferty nodded absently. In spite of his disagreement with Llewellyn about who was most likely to have murdered Clara Mortimer and his previous, confident response to the Parkview Apartment residents that he expected to make an arrest, the suspect he had had in mind hadn't been Harry Mortimer.

Although not usually one to look askance at a gift horse *or* its mouth, Rafferty couldn't help but wonder what had prompted Mortimer's confession. It couldn't have been encouraged by the fear that they were about to arrest him. How could it? Rafferty reasoned. He must know that all they had was circumstantial evidence – the circumstance that he had deceived them at first as to his identity and that he seemed likely to gain handsomely from Clara Mortimer's death.

Rafferty left it to Llewellyn to accompany Mortimer to his bedroom to supervise the packing while he further pondered this latest event.

It was true, he acknowledged, that Harry Mortimer had the perfect motive; Clara had been a wealthy woman in spite of the presumed depredations made by her feckless husband and daughter down the years. He had also had the means and the opportunity, all three strands of the case against him further strengthened by the suspect and belated alibi provided by Mortimer himself which had been backed by both his daughter and grandson. They were still awaiting confirmation or otherwise that as she claimed, Jane had been in the Laundromat at the time her mother was murdered. The Laundromat manager who she claimed had left a note on the door had gone off on holiday according to his employers and wasn't due back for another week. Did Mortimer know that this manager's return would reveal that Jane had again lied to them? And had this prompted him, for the first time in his life, to do the decent thing by his troubled daughter and take the rap for her?

It was a possibility, Rafferty thought. Though given Mortimer's previous careless abandonment of that same daughter, it was not a particularly likely one. Rafferty wondered if perhaps he was being contrary and Mortimer's confession was no more than the plain truth.

Certainly, Harry and Clara Mortimer had never divorced; if she *hadn't* made a will – which both Rafferty and Llewellyn now agreed was more than probable – Mortimer could expect to be in line for a substantial sum – even if he had to go through the courts to get it.

And yet . . . and yet . . . In spite of Mortimer's sudden confession, in spite of the circumstantial evidence, Rafferty still harboured doubts – and more than doubts – about Harry Mortimer's confession, and although his mind chased after elusive will-of-the wisps of evidence against suspects he felt more likely to be guilty of Clara Mortimer's murder, there was no gainsaying the fact that by the time Llewellyn returned with Mortimer, packed bag in hand, he was no nearer to finding convincing evidence against these suspects. Left with no alternative after Mortimer's confession, Rafferty knew he had to take the man into custody. After cautioning him and advising him of his rights, they brought Mortimer downstairs, put him in the back of the car and drove to the station.

But although Harry Mortimer's admission of guilt meant the case was over, Rafferty still felt there was unfinished business. And although, back at the station, he accepted the congratulations of his colleagues, he wasn't happy. Something about the case still *niggled* him. What was it?

Perhaps it was the timing of Mortimer's confession?

Why had he chosen to hold his hands up now? What event in his life could have encouraged it?

Rafferty's mobile rang and interrupted his thoughts shortly after they had brought Mortimer through to the charge room for processing. And as his sister, Maggie's, anxious voice echoed in his ear, all the doubts and questions about the murder investigation flew from his mind.

'I'm at the hospital, Joe,' she began in a strangely subdued voice that was so unlike his sister. 'It's—'

'Don't tell me something's happened to Gemma? Or little Rambo? What—?'

'No. Gemma and Rambo are fine. It's Abra. She's lost the baby.'

'Lost the baby? But she can't have.'

Illogically, he thought, but we haven't even made up our minds what we're going to do about it yet. This thought was followed by another – how did his sister even *know* about the pregnancy? Unless his ma—

But this line of thought hadn't proceeded far before his sister, who must have guessed the way his mind was working, interrupted.

'Abra's been spending a lot of time with us, Joe, with Gemma and the baby. She swore me to secrecy, which is why I couldn't let on, to you or Ma.'

That explained why Abra had never been home when he called at her flat, why she had never returned his increasingly desperate answerphone messages. Surely, she hadn't been at his sister's house while he'd been babysitting?

Again, his sister's voice broke into his unwelcome thoughts. 'Naturally, it came pouring out. Why didn't *you* tell us about the pregnancy, Joe?'

'I-I—'

Maggie interrupted his spluttered attempts to explain his less than heroic behaviour.

'Never mind. It's too late now. But Abra's very upset. You'd better get here as soon as you can. She's on the same ward that Gemma was on,' she told him.

'Right. Yes. Of course. I'll come now. Tell Abra . . . Tell her. No, I'll tell her myself,' he said before he ended the call.

What am I to tell her? he wondered as he whispered a brief explanation to Llewellyn before he raced off to the car.

Hesitantly, with a guiltily furtive air, Rafferty entered the side ward that Abra occupied. He glanced at Maggie, who sat by the bedside. She shrugged and shook her head.

Although he kissed Abra and asked her how she was feeling, she made no response. Hollow-eyed, she just stared ahead of her while more tears fell to mingle with the tracks of those that had fallen earlier.

'Abra? Sweetheart? Talk to me. Please don't shut me out again.'

She looked at him as if she didn't recognize him. 'Don't shut you out?' she repeated in a dull little voice from which all her previous sparkle had vanished. 'You shut yourself out when you made it clear that you didn't want our baby – *my* baby.' Even more dully, she added, 'You got your wish.'

Not knowing what he could do or say for the best, he simply reached for her hand and gripped it tightly. At least she didn't pull it from his grasp.

The quiet of the small side ward was broken as the voice of a little boy echoed along the corridor. The child could have been no more than three. He ran in to the ward and launched himself at a middle-aged woman in the bed by the door, shouting, 'Hi, Gwan, is me,' chased by his out-paced and furiously 'shushing' mother.

'Don't shout so, Jamie. I told you. You have to be quiet. This is a hospital. It's full of sick people.'

'Is Gwan sick, Mummy?'

'No, darling. She's just had a baby.' She lifted the toddler off the bed and held him over the glass crib. 'Take a look at your new uncle.'

Clearly astonished that he should have an uncle who was smaller than he was, the little boy stared down at the new infant. But whatever else it did, his astonishment silenced him and the small ward returned to the peace it had enjoyed before the child's arrival.

In the restored quiet, Maggie stood up. 'I'll leave you two alone. You need to talk.'

Rafferty wanted to beg her to stay. He didn't know what to say to this new, subdued Abra.

'I'll just be outside,' Maggie told him, as if, yet again, she had second-guessed him.

He nodded. 'Thanks, Mags. I appreciate you being there for Abra.'

The thought *somebody had to be* entered Rafferty's head.

When Maggie had gone, warily, Rafferty questioned Abra. 'Did the doctors say why you lost the baby?'

Abra gave a forlorn little shrug. 'Just one of those things, was what they said. It's not unusual, apparently. But why did it have to happen to our baby. *My* baby?' Again, she immediately corrected herself, before she burst into floods of noisy tears.

Rafferty put his arms round her and hugged her tight. 'Perhaps it was for the best,' he ventured. 'Often these things happen – or so I understand – because the baby hadn't formed properly.'

'I know that,' she muttered against his shoulder. 'They told me that. But they didn't seem to understand that that was even more upsetting to know. *Why* hadn't it formed properly? Is there something wrong with *me*?'

'Of course there isn't. The doctors would have said. Don't go blaming yourself, Abra.'

But it seemed she did blame herself. Of course she also blamed *him*.

Rafferty, relieved she had condescended to talk to him at all and desperate to make amends, asked her what he could do to gain her forgiveness.

She told him.

*   *   *

Rafferty got a not-unsympathetic Llewellyn on the phone and begged a favour before he went in search of the ward sister. As he had explained to Llewellyn, there were some things even more urgent than murder investigations.

He was aware, even if Abra seemed not to be, that foetuses of such short gestation didn't merit a birth certificate, never mind the funeral or death certificate which Abra seemed to expect him to organize.

Fortunately, the ward sister confirmed he was in time. Once he had explained what he wanted, she brought him along to the sluice room, pointed out the abortive foetus and left him to say his goodbyes as he had requested.

As soon as the ward sister had left, Rafferty hunted in his jacket pockets and found a large evidence bag. Gently, he eased the tiny foetus into it and hid it under his jacket.

Conscious he had badly failed Abra over the baby's short life, he was determined he wouldn't fail her at its death. He was certainly unable to bring himself to tell her that to the authorities who decided such things, a miscarried foetus of only a month or two's gestation wasn't considered a viable human being and did not merit certificates or a funeral.

The arrangements took a while, several visits, some more hurried phone calls and a few threats, but finally, they were in place.

Two hours later, he hustled Father Kelly and his righteous indignation into the nearest gents' toilet. But even the blustering Father Kelly, faced with Ma Rafferty's 'persuasion', evidently realized that protest was futile, so he soon stopped complaining and accepted the inevitable

'You can get ready in here, Father,' Rafferty told the priest. 'I'll just go and prepare Abra.'

Father Kelly and all his paraphernalia were Rafferty's make-amends 'gifts' to Abra. It was fortunate that he had arrived at the hospital in time to prevent the removal of the tiny, bloodied remains of their child.

He had even obtained a birth certificate; not a real one, obviously. But the computer-buff Llewellyn had certainly come up trumps in the short time available after Rafferty's desperate pleas had persuaded him to agree to some creative graphics on his computer. The birth certificate certainly had the look of the real McCoy, which was all that mattered.

The death certificate, somehow, he had felt unable to request. Perhaps if he hadn't been so quick to deny their child's existence, he wouldn't feel so constrained about faking this also.

He had even, with his ma's assistance – and owing to what blackmail, he didn't ask – managed to persuade Father Kelly to give the tiny remnants of their child a proper funeral Mass. They would have the full ceremony at another time, for obvious reasons. But today, he was to give a much shortened version for Abra's sake.

Rafferty checked quickly up and down the corridor to make sure there was no one in authority in sight before he hurried to the Gents, retrieved the robed-up Father Kelly and hustled him along to Abra's little ward before anyone in authority had a chance to spot them.

Once there, he pulled the curtains round the bed and whispered to Father Kelly that he would have to keep his voice down.

Dull-eyed at first, Abra's face slowly became more animated. She cried when she saw the tiny white coffin that Father Kelly had obtained from the local funeral director, which he had secreted in a large sports bag.

Rafferty wondered that no one had questioned the incongruity of such an item in the hands of the florid, overweight and evidently unsportsmanlike priest.

Although their child had not sufficient form to be actually dressed in the doll's frilly frock that stood in for a Christening robe that Rafferty had begged from his youngest niece, he handed it to Abra and she laid it tenderly over the barely-there remains of what should have been their child.

Then, on his knees, Abra's hands enfolded in his, Rafferty bowed his head for the Last Rites as the irrepressible old rogue, Father Kelly, intoned the solemn words.

It was fortunate they had such an obliging man for a parish priest, he mused as the priest droned on. Father Kelly loved sinners as his ma had reminded him. But as she had also remarked, of course Father Kelly loved sinners – wasn't the priest the greatest sinner in the parish?

Rafferty didn't know what sins the priest had committed, though it was clear his ma did and that was all that mattered. But old sinner or not, Father Kelly could be portentously solemn when the occasion demanded.

In a voice hushed with reverence, he intoned, 'He that is born of woman has but a short time to live . . . In the midst of life, we are in death . . . Earth to earth. Ashes to ashes. Dust to dust . . .'

Rafferty had found the little service upsetting and deeply moving. So, for that matter, had Abra, although, she, at least, seemed to find some solace in the old ritual.

As she said to him afterwards, 'Our child had life, even it if was only for a short time, within me. I needed to acknowledge that life. I needed the world, too, to acknowledge that our little Joseph had existed.'

Misty-eyed, Rafferty said, 'You called him after me?'

'Well, yes, of course. But you knew that already.'

She held out the fake birth certificate and handed it to him.

Rafferty took it and looked. Then he smiled. 'Of course I did. What else would we call our first-born son?' He sent up a silent 'thank you' to Llewellyn, his sensitive, computer-literate DS for thinking of this. Then he handed the paper back to Abra, before he took his last little gift out of his bag.

This final gift was a bottle of champagne, still chilled from its immersion in the bucket of ice in which it had made its journey to the hospital. And as he handed flutes to Abra and the suddenly bright-eyed Father Kelly, he said, 'It might be the Jews who believe that each death should be a celebration of life, but as a lapsed Catholic, it's a sentiment I can applaud.'

He poured the wine, first into Abra's glass, then into Father Kelly's, finally, into his own, before he raised his glass and said, 'To our son, Joseph, short though his life was. *L'chaim.*'

Abra and Father Kelly paused for only a heartbeat, before they clinked glasses and added, '*L'chaim.*'

Before the echo of their voices had died away, Rafferty sent up a tiny vow. Next time, he promised, next time, I'll do it right.

It was much later that night – after Father Kelly had departed with the tiny coffin that contained their child concealed in the sports bag, after Abra, with little Joseph's 'birth certificate' clasped to her chest, had finally fallen asleep – that Rafferty had returned to his flat. He had gone to bed and had eventually managed to quieten his mind after all the stresses of the day.

He had just begun to doze off, when his sleepy brain threw up a new thought about Clara Mortimer's murder. Her estranged husband's confession zoomed back to the forefront of his mind. But this time, Mortimer's confession sat in uneasy alliance with something else that brought a frown to his forehead. And he wondered why the incongruity of this now recollected evidence hadn't struck him before.

He was instantly wide awake again. He could only assume it was because he was at his most relaxed at the end of an emotionally fraught day that his brain finally released its grip on the golden nugget.

And although, as yet, he only had a misty grasp as to why the selfish Harry Mortimer had decided to make his unselfish 'confession', he now knew, almost for certain, that Mortimer *hadn't* killed his estranged wife. At least he thought he did.

But Rafferty believed that come the morrow, some serious questions were likely to confirm it. And as he recalled Llewellyn's reminder that to conclude the paperwork, they ought to interview Mrs Toombes's elusive fisherman husband, he felt confident that this need to revisit their apartment would provide sufficient excuse to question Mrs Toombes again and hopefully, this time, get her to tell them the truth.

Fifteen

Mrs Toombes, now she had her husband home, seemed far more relaxed and happy than she had been at their first meeting.

As Llewellyn and Rafferty entered the Toombeses' living room with its overloud TV, Rafferty knew his previous night's conviction that Mrs Toombes would repay further questioning had been correct.

Although they had, ostensibly, come to interview *Mr* Toombes in order to tidy up the paperwork, Rafferty was more than ever convinced that *Mrs* Toombes was the one to whom they should direct their questions.

While Mrs Toombes twittered around them, Rafferty wondered why he hadn't thought to bring up such an obvious question earlier in the case. On their previous visit to the apartment he had considered the TV too loud for comfort, but had thought no further on the subject. Now, though, as its loudness hit him again, he felt even more convinced he had the answer.

The difficulty, he thought, as Mrs Toombes ushered them into her living room, was to get her to admit it.

She introduced them to her husband.

At least, Rafferty assumed the man sitting with the broadsheet newspaper thrust before him as a protective measure against Mrs Toombes's endless twittering and the over-loud TV was *Mr* Toombes. But as the TV overrode his ears' hearing ability, he had to guess the man's identity.

Rafferty smiled a greeting and awaited clues.

Whoever the man was, he, at least, noticed Rafferty's protective wince and curled-up ear lobes, for he reached across for the zapper to turn the TV off.

Grateful for the sound of silence, his sensitivities at fever pitch, suspecting he was reaching critical mass in the current investigation, but newly awakened to the woman's own sensitivities, Rafferty asked, 'Mrs Toombes, you remember telling me about the man who rang your entryphone early on the morning of Mrs Mortimer's murder?'

'Yes, of course I remember,' she told him sharply. 'I told you before, young man, that I don't have a problem with my memory. How could I possibly forget the events of that day?'

Rafferty nodded at this and couldn't help but think her sharp rebuke about not having a problem with her *memory* was a defensive mechanism to camouflage her true problem.

'Now, I want you to think carefully,' he said, conscious of the need to speak as tactfully as possible about the problem he suspected she strove hard to conceal. 'Is it possible you misheard what the man said?'

'Certainly not. I know what I heard.'

Her defensive response encouraged his belief that he was right. But how to get her to admit it? Fortunately, he discovered as Mrs Toombes's husband lowered his newspaper that he didn't have to.

'Are you sure about that, my dear?' he asked his wife. 'You know what a trial you find that intercom.'

In an aside to Rafferty, he added, 'My wife's hearing isn't what it was, Inspector.'

Mr Toombes's laugh boomed out as he turned to his discomfited wife. 'Remember that time you misheard one of the neighbours on the phone?'

He turned back to Rafferty, ignoring his wife's frantic signals that he keep quiet. 'She thought he was selling something, but all he'd done was forgotten his key to the apartment block. It was summer holiday time and hardly anyone was home. The poor man complained to me afterwards that he had to hang around outside for two hours before another neighbour came home and let him in.'

'That was different,' Mrs Toombes protested. 'The man was a terrible mumbler.'

Mr Toombes shrugged, said, 'I never had any trouble understanding him,' and retreated behind his newspaper.

'Mrs Toombes?' Rafferty repeated. Gently, conscious that the fact her husband had embarrassed her was the more likely to encourage her to dig her heels in, he said, 'Your neighbour, Clara Mortimer, died a brutal death. I'm right in believing you want her killer caught?'

'Of course I do, young man. Why ever wouldn't I? We none of us can sleep safely in our beds till he's apprehended.'

'That's why I'm asking you to think very carefully. What you tell me now could make the difference between us catching her killer – or not. It's important.'

Mrs Toombes seemed torn between her unwillingness to admit to an affliction considered an elderly persons' one and her desire to do what was right.

Hoping to help, Rafferty repeated the words she had told him the man had said to her.

'Yes, that's right,' she confirmed. But her confirmation lacked her previous conviction. '"I ran, Esme" is what he said.' Belatedly, she admitted to the hearing difficulties her husband and the overloud TV had already revealed.

'The line was a bit crackly. I find these entryphones a bit of a trial, to be honest, as my husband had just told you.'

Mr Toombes broke in with another insensitive husbandly guffaw.

'A bit of a trial?' he repeated. To Rafferty he confided, in a loud aside, as if his wife, from her seat a yard from him, would be unable to hear him. 'She's as deaf as a post. We have to have the TV on so loud I'll be as deaf as she is before my next birthday. Surely you told the inspector that your hearing's not to be relied upon?' he demanded of his wife.

Humiliated, her carefully concealed poor hearing now out in the open, Mrs Toombes turned even more defensive. Earnestly, she appealed to Rafferty. 'So many people nowadays seem to slur their speech, don't you find, Inspector?'

As the supportive husband, with a 'Harrumph,' had once again retreated behind his newspaper, Rafferty found himself nodding sympathetic agreement at the same time as his heart began to race.

'Anyway, as I told you before, this man seemed to be looking for someone called Esme. I admit I wasn't sure that I had heard correctly, so, after I had told him there was no one here of that name, I was about to ask him to repeat what he had said. But I didn't get a chance. He just hung up on me. So rude. Isn't that so, Ernest?'

Mr Toombes sighed, shook his newspaper and turned over the page. 'As you say, my dear, but that's modern times for you.'

Rafferty sat forward. He tried to conceal his eagerness as he said again, 'I want you to think carefully, Mrs Toombes.'

This brought a worried look and another glance for guidance towards her husband.

But Mr Toombes must have sensed the glance for, once more, he determinedly retreated behind his newspaper with a lot more 'Harrumphing' that left no doubt she was on her own.

Rafferty sighed inwardly and asked, 'Is it possible that what the man *actually* said was . . . ?'

Immediately he had told her what he suspected the man had said, Mrs Toombes's face lit up as though someone had just turned on a lamp inside her head. She began to nod, delightedly.

Without even glancing towards her unsupportive husband,

she exclaimed, 'Of course. That must be it. I can see it now. It makes much more sense. But how *sad*. You are clever, Inspector, and you didn't even *speak* to him. I feel so foolish now. How ever did you guess?'

'There's no need to feel foolish,' Rafferty assured her. 'I had a murder to solve. You didn't. And it occurred to me that what that man said might just be the key to the case.'

And now that her husband and, sheepishly, Mrs Toombes herself had just confirmed his belated suspicions about her poor hearing, he knew his instincts had been right.

'I suspected the killer must have used some ploy to gain entrance to Mrs Mortimer's home, so I just let my mind play about with possibilities. Of course, now that I've been able to put this idea together with your evidence . . .' He broke off before his insensitive tongue ran away with him.

He didn't add that if Mrs Toombes had admitted when he had first questioned her that her hearing was impaired, he might have started wondering much earlier if what she had claimed the man had said was accurate, which might well have led him to a speedier solution.

But he had the solution now – and that was all that mattered.

'How sad' had been Mrs Toombes's response when Rafferty had queried whether the man who had rung her intercom could have actually said, 'Hi, Gran, it's me', rather than the 'I ran, Esme' that Mrs Toombes had previously insisted she had heard.

Naturally, she now assumed that one of Clara Mortimer's grandsons had killed her.

She was right, of course, but not in the way she had thought. For Rafferty believed Charles Ogilvie hadn't deliberately targeted his own grandmother. He believed the claim of his mother and sister that Ogilvie didn't even know his grandmother's new address.

When Rafferty had questioned Clara Mortimer's elder

grandson about his whereabouts at the time of her murder, Charles Ogilvie had seemed nervous, evasive; Rafferty had thought at the time that the young man had been trying to shield someone; his mother, for instance.

How wrong he had been, he realized, because it was now apparent that rather than Charles Ogilvie being the provider of protective alibis, it had been his mother and grandfather, the two feckless family members, who had together concocted an alibi in order to protect *him*.

Had Harry Mortimer feared they would learn the truth if they continued to question his sensitive and immature grandson? Was that what had prompted his 'confession'?

Rafferty had thought there must be something more; for, in spite of Mortimer's claim to having murdered Clara, Rafferty hadn't believed him. Why would the man who admitted to having led a totally selfish life suddenly sacrifice himself?

He had already pondered long and hard about Harry Mortimer, his confession and its timing. In spite of his protests about 'responsibility', Rafferty didn't believe that people like Harry Mortimer who had been selfish all their lives ever really changed – not unless some life-altering event wrought the alteration.

Nor had he understood why Jane must have agreed to allow the father she adored to sacrifice himself. It was only now, as he recalled Harry Mortimer's gaunt features and compared them to the well-fleshed groom he had been in his and Clara's wedding photograph on display in Mary Soames's home, that he began to wonder if the man was ill – terminally ill.

Was Mortimer making one grand gesture to make amends to his daughter and grandson for all his previous failures? It would explain his sudden character change.

The big, strapping man in the wedding photo that Mary Soames had shown them wasn't the same man at all. Harry Mortimer was now a gaunt shadow of his former self, his face as cadaverous as the corpse Rafferty was beginning to suspect Mortimer was soon to become.

Now, with the solution to the investigation in his grasp, Rafferty realized he had seen death in Mortimer's eyes. But it wasn't the death of his wife that he had seen there, but Mortimer's own.

And if he was right in his suspicions, there was one way to find out.

'But you can't arrest Charlie!' Jane screamed at them when Rafferty and Llewellyn revealed the reason for their latest visit. 'My father's already admitted he killed her.'

'And how do you know that, Mrs Ogilvie? Unless you agreed he would do so before he spoke to us? Before the disease that is killing him claimed him?'

'You know about that?' she asked in a shocked whisper, before she realized her mistake and broke off.

'You just admitted that you hadn't seen or spoken to your father since yesterday morning,' Rafferty pointed out. 'So unless you and he concocted this story between you before your father made his confession to us, I don't see how you could have known about it.'

Jane's eyes darkened as she searched frantically for a response.

At their accusation, Jane had thrust herself protectively in front of her eldest son as if she intended to provide a physical barrier. But now she moved aside, grasped the terrified-looking Charles's arm and dragged him forward, with the beseeching cry, 'Look at him. Look at my smart son. How can you think he would kill his own grand-mother?'

'I don't suppose he meant to,' Rafferty replied. 'But I believe he was desperate. He admitted to me himself that he had some debts.'

As he recalled the expensive mirror smashed to smithereens in the entrance lobby to Clara Mortimer's apartment, Rafferty remembered a conversation he had had some time previously with a member of the drugs squad. This man had told him that, in their paranoia, drug addicts developed an aversion to mirrors and often smashed them. It was as if, his informant had revealed, they were unable to stand the sight of their own weakness reflected back at them.

Mary Soames, it was, who had told him that Aurora's father, Earl Ray, had been a bad influence on the children; and so he *had* been, for Charles at least. Though Hakim could have been no more than four and protected by the innocence of his tender years, the same couldn't be said for Charles. So much older than his two half-siblings, he would have been at a vulnerable age when his mother took up with the bad lad drug dealer. What was more likely in that ill-run menagerie than that the boy would be encouraged to experiment with the drugs from which Ray made his precarious living?

Rafferty addressed his next remarks to Charles Ogilvie. 'I'd guess you owed money to some pretty nasty people. Drug dealers who were threatening violence if you didn't pay up. But you couldn't pay up, could you? You'd lost your job.

'In your desperation, you hit on the idea of robbing elderly ladies, people who were even more vulnerable than yourself, in order to get the money to pay the dealers off. But your victims needed to be not just elderly and vulnerable, but *wealthy* and vulnerable. What would be the point in targeting the elderly poor who had no more money than you had yourself?

'You found your answer in the private sheltered blocks in the town that catered for the well-off old folk of the area. Elmhurst's not that large; I imagine you soon realized there were no more than two or three such sheltered apartments worth targeting.'

Rafferty had noted Charles Ogilvie's trembling hands and generally washed-out appearance and had put it down to shock at his grandmother's violent death. Now though, put together with the rest, the young man's pallid looks made sense.

Rafferty turned back to Jane. 'You said your son wouldn't kill his own grandmother, but he didn't know Mrs Mortimer *was* his grandmother. You told me yourself that he didn't even know where she lived. Thanks to the family estrangement, he hadn't seen her since he was a young lad. And isn't it true what they say? That one old lady looks much the same as another, with their white hair, wrinkles and old-fashioned clothes?'

Rafferty took a stab in the dark. 'I imagine it was only when he saw the photo of himself that he realized the identity of the woman he had just killed.

'It must have been an awful realization,' he said to Charles. 'You loved her once. Maybe a part of you remembered the happy times you'd had with her. It must have made your current problems and lifestyle seem even more tawdry. Was it that which made you smash the mirror?'

Charles began to weep. And although his mother tried to get him to shut up, through the sobs that wracked his slim frame, he tried to justify his actions.

'I couldn't stand myself,' he admitted. 'After what I'd just done, that mirrored reflection brought me face to face with the reality of my life and what I'd become. I had to make it go away. Smashing the mirror seemed the only way.'

After further questioning, Charles Ogilvie broke down even more and admitted he had hit on the 'Hi, Gran, it's me' ploy as a means to gain entrance to such places as the sheltered Parkview Apartments block. He just rang bells and when an elderly lady answered, said simply, 'Hi, Gran. It's me.'

He told Rafferty that he hadn't tried this ploy when men answered the bell – he was bright enough to realize that on the whole, elderly men were far less sentimental about their grandchildren and wouldn't hesitate to challenge such a statement. But the elderly ladies, many of whom, because of modern marriage break-ups, to their regret, often saw little of their grandchildren, were far less likely to challenge him.

Unwilling to admit that they didn't recognize the voice of one of their own grandchildren who had become a stranger, they would seldom question him further.

It was a particularly clever psychological ploy. It played on people's anxieties, loneliness and sentimentality. It made use of the elderly ladies' natural worry that their seldom seen grandchild must be in trouble to turn up out of the blue. This worry, in turn, would bring another emotion, one even more likely to encourage them to open their doors – that, in trouble, their grandchild had turned to *them* for help – a thought no doubt helped along by joy at feeling useful once more.

Although he had yet to speak to Harry Mortimer again, either to question him further or tell him that his confession wouldn't save the boy, Rafferty suspected that Harry had discovered his grandson had been doing drugs and was deeply in debt to some seriously nasty people. Doubtless, he had suggested to Clara that, together, they might be able to rescue their grandson from the curse of drugs that gripped him.

Rafferty also suspected that Harry, in all innocence, had suggested he would speak to Charles and try to persuade him to go to see her, so that she could attempt to use the softer, grandmotherly words to persuade him from the wrong path he had taken.

But before he could do so, Charles's desperation had prompted him to try out his robbery ploy once again, with tragic results. Because Clara Mortimer would have been *expecting* her favourite grandson to turn up on her doorstep; which was exactly what he had done, of course. But what she hadn't understood was that Charles Ogilvie, far from being ready to seek help for his addiction and debts, was

merely continuing with the method he had thus far successfully hit on to enable him to feed both.

Charles Ogilvie admitted he had been drawn to the sheltered housing block confident that therein he would find at
least one elderly woman who would buzz him in when he
said the magic words: 'Hi, Gran. It's me.'

But this time the ploy had resulted in death and tragedy,
because as it turned out, Clara Mortimer wasn't the only
one in for a nasty surprise. As Charles confessed to Rafferty,
it had only been after he had hit the old woman and she
had fallen to the floor that he had realized why their conversation had been so mutually incomprehensible that he had
struck her in frustration.

As he had admitted, it had been then that he had noticed
the photograph that her body had been blocking from his
sight. Instantly, he had recognized the child he had been
and after a second or two puzzling out what the woman
whose flat he had come to rob was doing with a picture of
him, it was but the work of further moments for his memory
to tell him of the identity of the second person in the photo.

To his dawning horror, he had realized the other person
in the photo was his once-adored grandmother out on a
seaside jolly with her grandson. And that he had just
murdered her.

To his eternal shame, he told Rafferty, he had fled and
left his grandmother to die.

Rafferty was appalled by Charles Ogilvie's tale. But the
events he now had reason to believe had followed the
violence, somehow managed to appal him even more.

Given that he believed Charles's horrified denial that he
had dragged his victim round the room, Rafferty was left
with only one conclusion. Clara Mortimer, realizing she
was dying and to save her grandson from receiving the
punishment he deserved, had, somehow, managed to drag
her dying self round her living room, smearing her blood
as she went, in a desperate attempt to remove Charles's

fingerprints before she succumbed to the blow and loss of blood.

'Mr Mortimer.' Rafferty entered the cell. 'You're free to leave.'

'What?' Harry Mortimer stared at him, his eyes sunk back in his gaunt head. But—'

'We know you didn't kill your estranged wife.'

'But I *did*,' he insisted. 'By now you must have checked and learned how much money Clara had. She always hated the idea of writing a will. She was strangely morbid about the idea. You haven't found one, I take it?'

Rafferty shook his head.

'There you are then. It sounds as if I'm about to become a rich man. Money, Inspector, don't they say that's the greatest motivation of all for murder?'

Rafferty wasn't surprised this realization should be uttered in a flat tone that revealed such riches would bring Mortimer little joy.

He came further into the small cell. 'Your estranged wife's murder wasn't about money – or at least not in the way that you imply. We know what happened, Mr Mortimer. It's pointless you insisting on your guilt any longer. You should know that we've charged your grandson, Charles Ogilvie, with murder.'

At this news, Harry Mortimer slumped down on the cell's thin mattress. But the slumping only lasted a matter of seconds. Then he straightened himself and managed a terse rejoinder. 'Do I get to hear what evidence you think you have?'

Rafferty shrugged. 'I don't see why not.'

After he had explained the reason for his conclusions, Harry Mortimer once more slumped back, his face even more Mick Jagger-cadaverous than before.

'Convinced we can prove your grandson's guilt now, sir?' Rafferty asked.

Mortimer gave a defeated nod.

'Now, I'd like to ask *you* something,' Rafferty told him. After Jane's revelation, if only to satisfy himself, he wanted confirmation of his guess from Mortimer.

'Why did you make that confession? What possible reason could you have had? You were about to inherit a large amount of money or, at least, had reasonable expectations that you would. You had – and now still have, a rich and rosy future to look forward to. Even if you don't inherit and your daughter gets your late wife's money, I doubt she would see you go short.'

Harry Mortimer shook his head and began to laugh, though the laughter held more than a hint of the macabre about it.

'Of course, you don't know. There's no reason why you should, I suppose. I'm dying, Inspector. I've got six months, if I'm lucky. I decided to "confess" the day after I received the doctor's verdict. I was already "going down". I saw no reason why young Charlie should have to go down, too. If it achieved nothing else, I thought my confession would draw the police fire from him.'

Rafferty gave a slow nod at this. It was just as he had thought.

'All my life I've let down Charlie, my daughter, the two younger kids and Clara, too. I thought, approaching death, I could at least try to remedy some of the wrongs I had done them all.'

He shrugged. 'Call it guilt, if you will; guilt for how my daughter turned out, guilt for not being there sooner for Charlie. If I hadn't been selfishly self-indulgent all my life – having flings with other women, gambling, never taking any responsibility – Clara and me might have made a go of the marriage and remained together. Who knows, maybe if we had, she wouldn't have been so severe on Jane that she rebelled.

'I've put myself first all my life,' he told Rafferty. 'Attempting to take my grandson's guilt on to my own

195

shoulders was the first unselfish act in a totally selfish life. You could say I wanted one of my last acts on this earth to be a wholly unselfish one.

'I wanted to help my grandson. Can you blame me for that?'

Rafferty shook his head.

'I hoped the knowledge that he had murdered his own grandmother because of his drug habit might straighten him out.'

'Maybe it will in the short term,' Rafferty said. 'But do you think it would really help the lad in the long run to know he had got away with murder? And such a murder? To my mind, it would be more likely to increase his problems than lessen them. Maybe better to have him feel he'd received the due punishment of the law by serving a prison sentence for his crime; that way he might eventually manage to put it behind him, straighten himself out and start fresh. By taking the blame and confessing to his crime you'd have given him a double load of guilt to bear – not only his grandmother's murder, but your sacrifice of whatever remains of your life. Given that he was weak enough to begin taking drugs in the first place, do you really think he – or his shoulders – are strong enough for such burdens?'

Mortimer looked shaken by Rafferty's words. 'Perhaps not; I hadn't thought of it in that way.'

'Perhaps you should do so,' Rafferty said. 'But before you do, let's get you out of here. Your daughter's waiting for you.'

Mortimer blinked. 'You're letting me go? I assumed you'd charge me with wasting police time, at least.'

Rafferty shook his head. 'No, Mr Mortimer. In the circumstances, I think we have rather more time to waste than you have. Go back to your family and do your best to support each other while you still can.'

And as he led Harry Mortimer out, Rafferty knew he also would do well to take his own advice.

Epilogue

As Rafferty read Charles Ogilvie's confession in all its sad delusion and guilty rhetoric, he reflected that the killing of Clara Mortimer was a very *modern* murder; could such a tragedy really have occurred at any other time in history?

Modern times, with their split and broken families, gave so many people vastly different experiences to those of generations fifty, even thirty years earlier. In many ways, between modern lives and lives in the fifties there existed a gulf as great as that between the fifties and the Middle Ages.

The fifties' drugs of choice for the greater number had been beer and Woodbines, not the skunk, cocaine and ecstasy that brought their accompanying loss of self-control, delusion and paranoia.

No – Rafferty nodded to himself – this was a modern murder all right. Briefly, he wondered how many more such murders there would be. He suspected that in these days of 'my grandson, the stranger'; 'my brother, the stranger' and 'my husband, the stranger', such sad family murders would become ever more common.

But he had no time now to reflect on the sad experiences of the Ogilvie/Mortimer families; he had a sad event of his own to attend.

For today was the day of his baby's funeral and he was due to go and pick up Abra from his sister Maggie's home, where she had insisted on staying since her release from hospital.

After the funeral Mass, Abra, having still not forgiven him, chose Kitty's over Rafferty's company on the walk to the graveside. Rafferty's sister Maggie fell into step beside him.

She squeezed his arm and asked, 'How are you feeling?'

Rafferty shrugged. 'Much as you'd think. What about you? How are you getting on with Mrs Newson?'

'I'm not,' Maggie told him.

'Don't tell me you've come to blows already?'

'No. But that's only because she's not been round to see little Joey.'

Rafferty, about to bury his own little Joey, had been touched that Gemma should decide to name her son after him. But his sister's words astonished him so much that they almost succeeded in emptying his mind of all other thoughts.

'Not been round? Given Linda Newson's determination that she wasn't going to be shut out, I'd have thought it would take her getting knocked over by a bus for her *not* to insist on her "rights". Are you sure she hasn't been in an accident?' he asked. 'At the very least, she must be laid up with a bad dose of flu.'

Maggie shook her head. A faint smile played about her lips. 'No, it's not that. I suspect she's given into Wayne's emotional blackmail.'

She explained. 'Ma heard from one of her friends whose daughter knows the Newsons that young Wayne didn't like his mother visiting his son. Apparently, he feared he would get dragged in and persuaded to acknowledge his responsibilities. He didn't fancy that, so he gave his mother an ultimatum. It was either him or the baby. He told her if she didn't give up seeing little Joey, he'd go and live with his dad.'

Rafferty snorted. 'You'd think she'd be glad to get rid of the little git.'

He might have only met Wayne Newson once, but it was enough. That brief encounter had made clear to him that Wayne's mother had spoilt her son rotten.

'You and I might think "good riddance", Joe, but Mrs Newson thinks the sun shines out of Wayne. He's the pride of his mother's heart. Anyway, she's decided to stick with the child in the hand, so to speak. Of course, she didn't admit any of this to me. Still, it's a relief to think she won't be ringing my doorbell several times a week, demanding "her rights" to see little Joey.'

Rafferty, thinking of his own lost child, observed, 'Still, it must be upsetting for her, Mags. How would *you* feel if you couldn't see your first grandchild?'

'You're right. Of course, you're right.' Maggie sighed. 'It's just that I've been so caught up in the demands of the baby and consoling Gemma and Abra, who have both been inclined to be weepy, that I haven't been able to spare Mrs Newson much thought. I'll send her some of the latest snaps of him and drop a note in to let her know how well he's doing.'

Feeling guilty that *his* behaviour towards Abra should have served to increase his sister's burdens, Rafferty managed only a weak. 'That's the spirit, sis,' just as they reached the graveside.

Father Kelly waited for the assembled mourners to settle, then opened his prayer book.

'In the midst of life we are in death . . .'

Rafferty, who had sidled furtively along the line of mourners, put one hand round Abra's waist. He was relieved not to be rebuffed. And as he stood at the tiny graveside and listened to Father Kelly read from his prayer book for Joe Junior's funeral, with the other hand, he fingered the black armband.

As the tiny coffin was lowered, Rafferty said his sad goodbyes to the little son he had, too late, come to love. It was only when Abra gripped tightly on to the hand round her waist that Rafferty knew he had a second chance both with Abra and parenthood. He meant to make the most of both.

This first world edition published in Great Britain 2004 by
SEVERN HOUSE PUBLISHERS LTD of
9–15 High Street, Sutton, Surrey SM1 1DF.
This first world edition published in the USA 2005 by
SEVERN HOUSE PUBLISHERS INC of
595 Madison Avenue, New York, N.Y. 10022.

British Library Cataloguing in Publication Data

Evans, Geraldine
   Bad blood. - (A Rafferty and Llewellyn mystery)
   1.   Rafferty, Detective Inspector (Fictitious character) - Fiction
   2.   Llewellyn, Sergeant (Fictitious character) - Fiction
   3.   Police - Great Britain - Fiction
   4.   Detective and mystery stories
   I.   Title
   823.9'14 [F]

ISBN 0-7278-6156-5

Typeset by Palimpsest Book Production Ltd.,
Polmont, Stirlingshire, Scotland.
Printed and bound in Great Britain by
MPG Books Ltd., Bodmin, Cornwall.

BAD BLOOD

Geraldine Evans

BAD BLOOD